THE CHRISTMAS PLAYBOOK

S. MASSERY
S.J. SYLVIS

A NOTE FROM THE AUTHORS

Dear reader,

We hope you enjoy The Christmas Playbook, which features beloved characters from our Shadow Valley U series (specifically, Heart of Thorns). This book is a mug of peppermint mocha (with whipped cream and sprinkles) in a hot tub in the middle of a blizzard. The perfect holiday recipe.

Happy reading!

xoxo,
    Sara & S.J.

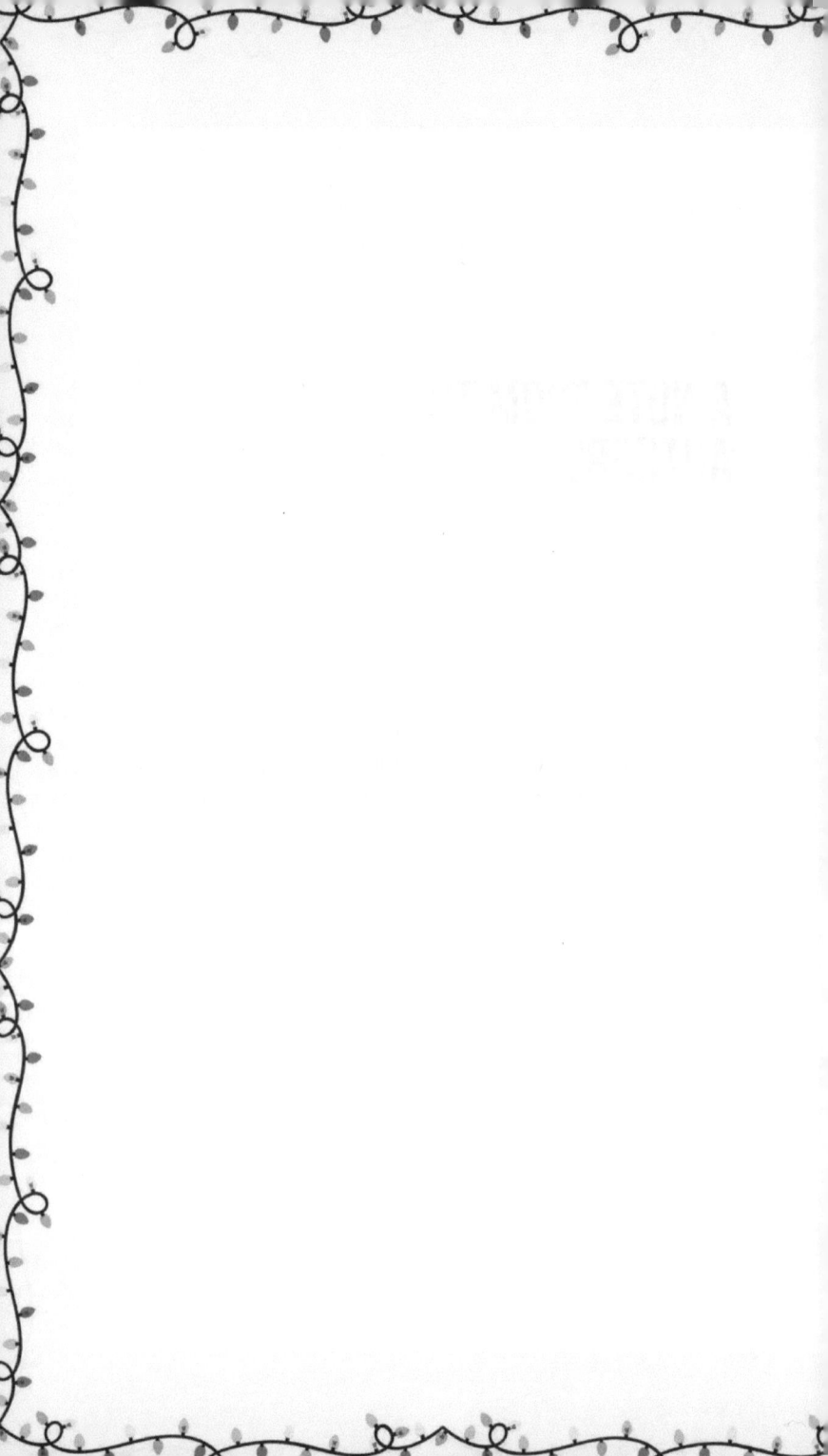

CHAPTER 1
RHYS

"MOM, IT'S GONNA BE OKAY." I zip my suitcase closed, hoping the sound is definitive enough. "I spend every holiday with you guys. This is our last big hurrah as a group before we disperse and never see each other ever again. Meanwhile, I'll see you for Easter. Fourth of July. Labor Day! Thanksgiving—"

"Okay, okay," my mother relents. "I get where you're coming from, baby, really. I'm just going to miss you. And I'm worried you're going to break your ankle at a ski resort. I know you. An injury would be gutting for your dreams."

She has a fair point—or she would if I wasn't a proficient skier. I've been on the slopes since I was barely old enough to walk. It's an excellent way to stay in shape, and I think my mother was desperate, at the time, to find some way to burn off my energy.

I love skiing. I love my best friends. I *hate* that we only have one semester left together, and then we all face the unknown.

My best friend in the entire world, Cassius Thorne—he goes by Thorne to everyone except his girlfriend—is going to be drafted. It's inevitable. I'd even bet money on him being in the top five picks.

Me? A little less certain.

I'm good, don't get me wrong. But am I NFL-level great?

One can only hope.

Either way. Thorne, and Briar, the aforementioned girl-friend, are both very confident in my ability to impress people.

No, wait, it's my ability to catch a ball that they believe in.

And maybe the rest will follow…

"I'll call you on Christmas Day, okay? We'll do a video call so you can see that I'm perfectly whole and intact." I crack a smile, even though my mom can't see me. "Just one holiday."

She makes a noise in the back of her throat. "I will hold you to that, Rhys."

"I know you will." I heft my suitcase off the bed and glance around the room. I've got everything I need—snow-boarding attire, of course, plus sweaters and jeans, socks, underwear, boots. Swim trunks for the private hot tubs, advertised as being on the back porch of every personal, private cabin.

Briar made sure to entice me with that, waving the brochure in my face over lunch one day. I was already sold on the idea, but I let her think *that* solidified it. So she took care of booking everything, and now…

It's go-time.

I drag my suitcase and backpack downstairs. Thorne is already in the living room, his luggage and Briar's by the door.

"Where's B?" I ask him.

He shakes his head. "On the phone with Marley. They're having some crisis over outfits."

My eyes bug out. *Women*, honestly. We're going to be in ski jackets the whole time—or in the hot tub. What else is there to think about?

The anticipation sings through me, and I pivot fast. Thorne may know better, but I…

Learning.

Always learning.

I march back upstairs and hammer on Thorne's door—more warning than I ever give him—then twist the knob and shove it open.

Briar is in the process of putting on a sweatshirt. The thing is over her head, her arms raised in the sleeves, and she looks… well, ridiculous is the first word that comes to mind.

I snicker, and she whirls around. She manages to drag it down, and the glare that awaits me is priceless.

"Thorne said you were having an outfit crisis." I gesture to her sweatshirt. "I'd agree."

"Shut up, asshole."

I grin. "It's time to go. We've got powder to plunge."

Her nose wrinkles. "Please never say that again."

"I won't if you get your butt in the car." I rap my knuckles on the door, which I probably should've done before I flung it inward. "Right now. Let's go."

Briar shakes her head at me and grabs her purse. I follow her downstairs then corral Thorne up and into the car.

Aaron, our football team's center, and his girlfriend, Willow, are meeting us at the airport. Plus Jack—another teammate—and his girlfriend, Marley. And Lydia and her boyfriend. Marley and Lydia are Briar's besties.

So, yes, you read that right. I'm the only single person on this trip.

But it's fine. I'm happier for it. I'll get a bed all to myself—unless I find a snow bunny to entice into it. I'll be able to let loose and have fun.

It's not a big deal at all. I could've found someone to invite if I wanted, but I didn't.

Don't.

Doesn't matter.

Away we go!

CHAPTER 2
MIRA

WE COULD GIVE the McCallister family a run for their money. I'm not sure if it's the scent of Christmas in the air, or the twinkling lights on the airport tree, but I'm pretty sure we're in the running to create another *Home Alone* movie—only our family is *worse*.

I may even petition for my name to be changed to Kevin because he and I are more alike than ever.

The forgotten child lost in the middle of pure fucking chaos.

"What's the name for your order?"

I glance at the barista and hardly contain a laugh when I say, "Kevin."

His brows cave for a second before he decides he doesn't care to ask and writes the name on the cup.

I squeeze past the bystanders, who are also waiting for their coffees while anxiously checking their watches for the time.

What is it with airports and everyone always being late?

My case is an exception, of course. I shouldn't have expected anything different when my sister walked up with two togo cups full of coffee and neither of them were for me.

"Oh, shoot. Sorry, Mira. I forgot to order you one."

I mean, really? She gets free coffee from me on a weekly basis from the café I work at, and she can't order me one at the airport?

She even managed to order coffee for Marcus. He probably got fifteen hours of precious teenager sleep. He doesn't need it to survive like the rest of us.

My phone has three texts from Rachel telling me to *hurry up.* I send her a middle finger emoji and shove my phone back into my bag.

"Kevin?"

I turn and stare behind me but quickly realize *I'm* Kevin, which would explain why the barista is staring at me.

"Oh, right! Thank you."

I suck half my latte down before making it back to the gate. My family sticks out like a sore thumb. Everyone, including myself, is gawking at the wildness occurring. There are so many of us that we nearly fill all the seats on the plane.

Okay, that's dramatic.

But still.

Rachel, the eldest of my siblings, stands beside her husband while he wrangles my nephew back into the stroller. Cammie, the second eldest, is making out with her fiancé behind the trash cans as if no one can see them. Then there are my two stepbrothers from my father's second marriage. Yeah, we're one of *those* types—where my father and mother divorced, remarried different people, and now we're just one big, happy, dysfunctional family. My stepbrothers' wives are both pregnant at the same time, unplanned—or so they say. My mom is fussing over the baby of the family, Marcus, who is taller than all of us. Then there's my stepdad, chatting away with my father who has long lost Eliza, my stepmom, because she's made her way over to Rachel to help her with Liam, the screaming toddler I mentioned from before.

The only benefit of going to Big Bear Ski Resort for our

annual Christmas trip is that I get my own cabin for the first time ever.

Never mind the fact that it's because they forgot to make sure I had a bed for myself. In an attempt to make things right, my stepdad booked me my own.

Marcus continues to dish out bribes to get me to give it up, but I refuse.

What teenage boy needs an entire cabin for himself?

The baby of the family will do just fine rooming with Mom and Jeff.

"There you are."

Rachel slides up beside me, and we both watch Tom, her husband, and Eliza, try to soothe Liam.

"Why does your coffee say Kevin?" Her jaw drops. "Did you steal someone's coffee, Mira?"

"No." I roll my eyes. "The barista misheard me." *God forbid I step a toe out of line.*

Despite the mayhem that occurs when we're all together, everyone in my family is pretty dang successful.

Except me.

Whether they've found their soulmate, attended some prestigious college, have a 401k, or a stable, well-paying job, they're all doing great. Even Marcus has been offered a full ride to the same university that my father attended.

Then there's me—the one who's still trying to figure it out. Whatever *it* is. Which is exactly what everyone says if I come up in conversation.

So what if I make scant money at the café, serving coffee?

"What do you mean he misheard you?" Rachel squints.

I shrug. "Kev-in, Mir-a. Two syllables."

Rachel scoffs, and I think I'm going to have to just tell her I stole the coffee so she'll move past it, but then I follow her line of sight.

Cammie and Andrew are practically dry humping, and it takes everything in me not to laugh.

"Dad is going to lose it," Rachel mutters.

"No, he isn't." I sigh. "He'll probably turn to me me and say, *'When are you going to find a boyfriend? Can't you be more like Cammie and get pregnant at an airport?'*"

Rachel snorts, and half our family looks at us.

"Cammie's pregnant?" Thomas asks.

Great.

"What? No." I shake my head at my stepbrother.

Rachel silently laughs under her breath.

"A little help?" I beg quietly.

"You're on your own."

What a bitch.

"I'll babysit for free," I hiss.

"Done." Rachel steps forward and points at me with her thumb. "Mira stole some guy's coffee."

My jaw slacks. "What? No, I didn't!"

"Is there a Kevin around?" my father shouts. "Is there a Kevin missing his coffee?"

If someone takes this coffee from my hand…

"Mira, just because you work at a café doesn't mean you can just help yourself to other people's drinks." My mom sighs.

My face is blank.

She gives me a disappointed look and turns away.

Our boarding group is called over the speaker, and I breathe a sigh of relief.

One three-hour flight and a quick shuttle to the resort stands between me and peace and quiet. Maybe I can figure out what to do with my life all alone in my warm, cozy cabin with nothing but my family's disappointment lingering around to fill the empty space.

CHAPTER 3
RHYS

IT TAKES *FOREVER* to get to the resort. From the drive, to the flight to California, to the *resort* in Big Bear, by the time we arrive, I am ready to jump out of my skin.

"Who would've thought Southern California would have good skiing?" I mumble.

Everyone ignores me. But we went from no snow and zero elevation to *all the snow*. The roads are clear, but the piles from the plow trucks on the sides of the road are taller than me, easy. It makes me want to leap from the vehicle and cannon-ball into them, but I refrain.

We park the two SUVs outside the main lodge, and we all go inside to check into our private cabins. The front desk girl seems a bit frazzled by all of us at once, but after signing paperwork and swiping credit cards, she hands out our keys with a cartoon map of the resort. It even has the different lifts and trails labeled for when we hit the slopes.

"There are parking spots at each cabin," she advises us. "We have a few different restaurant options here at the lodge, including our world-renowned restaurant at the top of Topher's Peak. All the information is in the binder in your cabin. Enjoy your stay!"

Thorne parks at his cabin, and we all pile out. His and Briar's cabin is close enough that I won't have to hike far to mine. Judging by the brass number nailed beside the door, I'm only one away. I, along with my friends, pull my luggage from the trunk.

"So, what are we gonna do now?" I ask. "Besides like, settling in…"

They exchange a glance that says they're probably gonna bone as soon as they're alone.

Great.

"Never mind." I roll my eyes. "You two have fun."

I trudge away, my arms full. The cabin key is in one of my pockets, but that's a problem for when I get to the porch.

"See you for dinner?" Thorne shouts behind me.

"Yep!"

Two minutes later, I climb up the steps to my new home for the week. I stomp the snow from my boots on the porch, which seems disappointingly bare. There's just a welcome mat. The one with the hot tub and rocking chairs, as advertised, must be in the back. Facing one of the runs, I hope.

There's no better people-watching than seeing inexperienced skiers wipe out, and that's just a fact.

Juggling my bags, I unlock the door and step in. The fireplace is already going, the flames crackling. I feel for a light switch, and the room suddenly illuminates.

There's a little kitchenette, a couch, a television. The bed seems warm and cozy, piled with blankets, in the corner.

I set my stuff down out of the way. It's a leftover habit from my parents' house. They hated when the kids would come inside and immediately drop their shoes, bags, whatever. The constant, *Put it in your room, Rhys!* got old by the time I turned seventeen.

After I move my luggage and ski bag to the far wall, by the dresser, I hurry to the drapes pulled across what I *hope* is a sliding glass door.

It is.

And there, in prime condition, is a hot tub.

"Halle-fucking-lujah."

I'm not messing around. I pluck one of the towels from the bathroom and strip out of my clothes. I could go for a beer or something, too. That might make this even better. But I am too excited to test out the tub. I wrap the towel around my waist and step outside, closing the drapes and then the sliding door behind me.

They had it closed, and I can only imagine it's to keep the chill out. Besides, enough light is filtering into the cabin through the windows. And the fire is doing a great job of making it cozy inside.

Anyway.

I push the lid off the tub and start the bubbles, barely suppressing my gleeful cackle. Just beyond the wooden railing is one of the trails, and even as I watch, a few snowboarders fly past.

Nice.

That'll be us tomorrow, crushing the slopes.

When the coast is clear, I shed the towel—folding it neatly and dropping it on one of the chairs—and hop into the tub.

Hot water immediately encases me, and I let out a groan. Perfection.

Fucking perfection.

The cold air makes the water seem even hotter, and I run my hands through the bubbles. I position myself with a view of the people coming down around the corner on the slopes, immediately locking on to a couple that seems to be struggling. They're flailing, a mess of ski poles and limbs.

I snicker.

It's wrong, yeah, but if they were seriously hurt, I would definitely get out and help them. I'd just, you know, take some pictures first.

Ah, hell. I left my phone inside.

I debate for a moment, then shrug. I don't need it. We're here to disconnect, and I should content myself with people-watching. The jets at my back are doing a great job loosening the tension there.

I already told my parents I had arrived.

Shit, no, I didn't.

Okay, it's fine, another hour or so won't kill them or me. I close my eyes, sinking lower until my chin brushes the water.

This is relaxation, this is peace.

This is…

Boring.

Boring!

Do people really just sit here and *chill?*

I don't know how long I last, but it's probably not long. I grimace and climb out, forgoing the towel to just sprint back inside, grab my phone, and return to the delicious water.

I jerk open the sliding door and whip aside the drapes. Water droplets roll off me, and I don't notice the open front door until I'm four steps inside.

Someone hauls a suitcase inside, their back to me, and I freeze. It's a girl.

Why is a girl coming into my cabin?

Is this a joke from Thorne and Briar?

Someone thought I'd be lonely for Christmas and found me a—

She turns and her gaze snaps to me.

Namely, my naked body.

Shit, I'm fucking naked!

She screams.

I scream, too, because that seems to be the appropriate response.

"I have a weapon!" she shouts, lunging for her bag.

"I don't!" I yell back, torn between raising my hands in surrender or covering myself. "Get out of my cabin!"

She pauses mid-search and slowly pushes her hair out of her face.

"Rhys?"

I stop and stare at her harder. She's not someone tagging along with our group, is she? I didn't want a jersey chaser coming with me. I could've had my pick, probably, but I wanted some freaking alone time.

Nope.

Recognition filters in too fast, and my body does this weird, swooping flush.

The heat from the fire is getting to me. I slowly cover my dick with both hands, because it's reacting, too.

Unfortunately.

My eyebrows hike, and I stare. This is impossible. She…

"Mira Winters," I say faintly.

She nods once. Just a jerk of her chin. Her hair swings again, obscuring her face. She glances over her shoulder at the open door, and I rush for my forgotten clothes. I yank my boxers and jeans into place, ignoring how the fabric drags over my wet skin.

By the time she looks back, I'm more decent than a second ago. But… *Mira Winters.*

We were neighbors in middle school.

That feels like a lifetime ago. And right now… she's definitely all grown up. No more braces—for either of us—or awkward spots of acne. Well, for me.

Damn.

"This is my cabin," Mira says.

That shatters any illusion that this was planned by my scheming best friend. Not that he would know who she was, but still. She and I were *tight.* Besties. As close as two twelve-year-olds could be anyway.

"So…" She frowns. "Can you get out?"

CHAPTER 4
MIRA

WHY IS MY LIFE A JOKE?

Rhys Anderson, my old neighbor, my old pal, my old *crush*.

I pinch myself to see if I'm dreaming, which only forces his eyebrows to cave in farther. Unfortunately for the both of us, this isn't a dream.

"Uh…" He glances around the cabin, as if he's searching for cameras, as if we're on some prank show. "This is my cabin, actually."

The hell it is.

I stomp my foot like a brat and cross my arms over my coat. "Listen," I start off with an even-tempered voice, but as soon as Rhys flicks his eyebrow, irritation rushes through me. "I've been on an airplane with my insane family for over three hours, then I was forced to sit in a car between my gigantic teenage brother, who took up more than half the seat, and my two-year-old nephew, who screamed the entire ride up this mountain."

I honestly think I might have lost hearing in my right ear. That, right along with my freaking mind.

"And?" Rhys is confused, and I'm annoyed.

"And get out! This is my cabin." I jingle the keys in front of his face, refusing to gape at his naked chest.

Rhys Anderson is no longer a boy with lanky limbs and random patches of facial hair. He's *all* man now, and it's hard to pretend like he's not. I didn't keep up with him after we moved away from one another, but I think I remember Marcus saying that Rhys was drafted for the pros.

He'll die when he realizes one of his heroes is here.

Rhys casually walks over to the table and swipes up a pair of keys of his own. He's no more than a foot away from me before he holds up his set and mimics my previous jingling.

"Looks like we're roomies, Frostbite."

An annoyed sigh falls from my mouth. Really? My old nickname?

"No."

I spin on my boots and head for the door.

Absolutely not.

I am *not* spending my entire ski trip being put down by my family only to come back to my cabin to share it with none other than Mr. Successful himself—Rhys Anderson.

No matter how insanely hot he is.

"Hot tub is this way. Where are you going?" Unfortunately, Rhys's voice doesn't fade the closer I get to the check-in desk.

He follows closely behind, asking me all sorts of questions.

None of which I answer.

How have you been?

Where do you live now?

Are you still obsessed with Justin Bieber?

Do you have a boyfriend? Or girlfriend? Single?

"Excuse me," I say sweetly to the girl at the desk. She is less overwhelmed than a little while ago when my family arrived in full chaos. "I think there has been a mistake."

"A mistake?" she asks, cheeks turning pink.

"I think you might have double-booked us." I point to Rhys, who *thankfully* covered up before following me in the snow.

The girl quickly pulls up something on the computer while Rhys and I stand side by side in awkward silence.

Well, awkward for me.

He seems cool, calm, and collected. His long fingers tap against the desk slowly as he observes the reception area with a content expression. He's nearly two feet taller than me now, and his shoulders are so much broader than when we were preteens. I feel small beside him.

"Oh my God," the girl mutters.

That's never good.

She stares at me with wide eyes. "We did double-book you."

Why does she seem so panicked by this?

Just give him a different room.

"That's fine." Rhys leans his elbow on the receptionist desk. "You can give Mira here a new cabin." He pauses. "Unless it's nicer than the one we're currently in. In that case, I'll switch."

I gasp and throw my elbow into his side.

He grunts at the same time a smile slides onto his face.

"You don't understand," the girls voice shakes with anxiety. "There are no more rooms available."

My whole body heats.

"What?"

Rhys makes a face, but he's quick to brush the issue off. "So, you're saying we need to share. Do we get a discount?"

I shoot him a glare.

"What? No, we won't *share*," I argue.

His eyebrows rise. "Do you have somewhere else to stay? Because I'm sure as hell not staying in any of my friends' cabins. They fuck like rabbits."

Just then, I hear a familiar laugh.

I glance over my shoulder at my two older sisters and quickly turn back to Rhys. His eyebrows furrow once again.

"Well?" he asks.

To stay with Rhys or to stay with one of my family members?

As I teeter between two impossible choices, I listen for either of my sisters' voices to get closer.

Shit.

"What are the chances that Mira self-combusts while we're here, with Mom and Dad asking her what her plans are every five seconds?" one trills.

"Between that and Eliza asking if she has a boyfriend or is interested in anyone? Yeah, I give it two days before she shouts something and stomps off to her cabin."

"Wanna make a bet?"

Rhys's gaze shifts from me to my sisters and then back to me. It's obvious he overheard them, and now I want to die.

My face heats, and I stare at the center of his chest.

This trip has hardly begun, and I'm already having a shitty time.

A bet? They're literally betting on what'll make me self-combust first? The implication that I'm unsuccessful in life or the talk of my nonexistent dating life? Both are touchy subjects because it's obvious that I'm the black sheep of the family.

Anger brews inside my chest, and I grit my teeth together.

"Marcus swears she'll be single forever." *Laughter.* They're right behind us.

That's the final straw.

I catch Rhys's eye mid-spin to my sisters, and I pray he plays along.

"Marcus is wrong." I lean back against Rhys's hard chest and smile deviously at my sisters. "I'm not single."

CHAPTER 5
RHYS

WELL, that fucking escalated quickly.

One minute, my mouth is opening, and I'm telling the receptionist that Mira and I can share the cabin. Which, for the record, is one of my more impulsive decisions. I kind of regretted it immediately, but her shocked expression was worth it.

Plus, I meant what I said—there is no way in hell I'm third-wheeling in my friends' cabins. Aaron and Willow are loud as shit. Don't ask me how I know. The vision of me sleeping with a pillow stuffed over my face flashes before my eyes. And Thorne and Briar? Still in the honeymoon phase, honestly. They probably concocted some bullshit rule about no clothes in the cabin.

I love Thorne, but I do *not* need to see his dick.

And he'd punch me if I accidentally saw Briar's tits.

But then—but *then*—Mira's sisters strolled into the lodge. I remember them, and I'm not too surprised by their catty conversation. A pang of empathy rolls through me. If I were her, I wouldn't want to share a cabin with them. Not after her outburst about being squished between a huge teenager and a two-year-old.

That sounds like the opposite of a good time.

Her gaze flicks to mine as she spins toward her sisters. I rotate with her, and she leans on my chest. Her body heat goes straight through the thin shirt I snagged on the way out the door.

"Marcus is wrong," she says to them. "I'm not single."

I barely bite back my gasp. She has a boyfriend? Then why the fuck is she leaning on—*oh*.

She's referring to *me*. This is not good. She's lying through her teeth, and I have half a mind to out her immediately just on the principle of the matter.

So why the fuck does my hand automatically go to her hip? My hand is huge against her, splaying across her abdomen.

The sisters' expressions drop, their eyebrows lifting. They don't even seem ashamed that they were overheard. The fact that there's not an ounce of guilt in their expressions goes straight through me.

What kind of monsters have they turned into?

Yeah, they were always brats. They shunned Mira because she was a little awkward.

Okay, a lot awkward. But that's why we got along. We were nerds together. We played alien cowboy space drifters—a made-up game that involved pretend guns and sprinting around our backyards. Her siblings would never.

Her parents didn't pay attention to her much either, come to think of it.

I refocus on Mira's sisters. Their names are escaping me, but I don't know if Mira wants to out me as the ex-boy-next-door. It might be too cliche, then she'd have to deal with *that* ridicule.

Besides, I look different. I grew a few feet, gained fifty pounds in muscle, lost the baby face…

"You have a boyfriend," one of them says in disbelief. It's the taller of the two. She's stick-thin, and she may as well have just stepped out of a ski magazine. Her gaze darts to my face, then sweeps down my body.

I've been inspected before, but never with such skepticism.

"Is that so hard to believe?" Mira asks.

My fingers flex, but I have no idea what the appropriate response is.

"Well…" The shorter, curvier one frowns. "It's just that you've never actually mentioned him."

"Can you blame her?" I rumble. "You both look like you're sucking on lemons."

Mira tries to cover her laugh with a cough, but I see right through her. I shuffle her to the side and put my arm over her shoulders. She's so much shorter than me that she tucks right in, like she was made for this spot.

Her arm comes around my waist.

"If you'll excuse us, I promised Mira three earth-shattering orgasms before dinner." I wink at her evil sisters.

They flush, which is a success in my book. I guide Mira away from them fast, propelling her forward. Back outside. Down the walking path back to our cabin.

Our cabin.

As soon as they're out of sight, Mira worms out from under my arm. She speeds on ahead, surprisingly fast for being so short. I lengthen my stride and catch up, resisting the urge to drag her to a halt to hash this out.

I can wait a few minutes.

The questions bubble up inside me, though. Like *what the fuck, Mira?* And *why did you do that?* And *how long is this ruse going to last?*

We make it inside, and I kick off my shoes. I grab her suitcase, which was abandoned right in the doorway, and drag it farther in. I set it next to my bags by the dresser. When I turn to face her, she's shed her jacket and glares at me from the middle of the cabin.

"Why are you staring at me like that?" I question. "You just told your sisters I'm your boyfriend."

Her jaw works, but she doesn't reply.

"Why did you do it?"

"You heard what they said."

I roll my eyes. "Yeah, I did. It was mean of them."

"It's nothing new either."

I know. I haven't seen her in years, not since we moved away from that neighborhood, but it doesn't matter. A tiger doesn't change its stripes, and clearly, emerging into adulthood didn't put Mira on even footing with her siblings.

"What do you want?"

"Three earth-shattering orgasms," she jokes.

God, please be joking.

I can't fuck her. Not that I would have to do that to bring her to a screaming climax… or three. I've got a magic tongue, and not just for talking. Or eating ice cream.

In fact, every ice cream cone I've devoured in my life has been in preparation for eating pussy. Just saying.

"Strip, then," I say.

She freezes. "Um—"

She was definitely joking. Oh, her cheeks are turning red. This is going to be fun.

"Relax, Frostbite." I chuckle. "I knew you were kidding."

"Oh, good." She relaxes. She even uncrosses her arms. "So…"

I take a seat on the edge of the bed. My traitorous mind goes straight to what her body will look like naked. Sharing a cabin with her *without* seeing it is… delusional. Right?

I'll get to see her naked, *right, Universe?*

Gosh, I'd turn in every fucking karmic brownie point I've ever earned to make that a reality. And it's not just because now I'm imagining what she tastes like. I've just been complaining about my friends getting laid for the whole trip, and I thought I'd have a cabin to myself to hook up with a random chick on vacation with her family…

But now one's going to be living in here, and that's simultaneously hot and a cock block.

"We should discuss this," she mutters.

My eyebrows hike. "Yeah? Maybe in the hot tub?"

"Did you bring swim trunks or—?"

"The nakedness was an impulse," I grumble. Like telling her we could share this cabin, which suddenly feels like it's a thousand degrees. "Don't worry, Frostbite, it won't happen again."

She's still beet red, but she shakes it off and goes to the little table. She drags out a chair and motions for me to sit across from her.

I do, angling my seat so I can kick out my legs. I rest my forearm on the table and drum my fingers, my gaze resting on her face.

Similar and different. Grown up.

Pretty.

No—beautiful. Blue eyes, long blonde hair, pink lips. She's not wearing makeup, but it doesn't fucking matter.

"Okay. So, um, my family will no doubt all know that I have a boyfriend by now." She can't face me. "Which means I either come clean to *all* of them that I lied, or…"

Or, I go along with it.

"What kind of commitment are we talking about, here?"

She lights up when I don't immediately write it off. Color me intrigued.

"Dinners, probably. At least two. We're here until January second. When do you…?"

"Same."

"Okay. Right. So, a couple dinners, just to satisfy their curiosity. I can make up something if you have plans with your friends. Um… skiing, too? A few times, just to show them that we're doing stuff together."

"I snowboard." I tilt my head. "That's not a problem, is it?"

"I… no. I rented a snowboard, too."

My eyebrows have a life of their own, because they shoot up. "When did you learn how to snowboard?"

"I can get by." She scratches at her neck. "We always come here. It's our Christmas tradition. And every year, I get snowboarding equipment and…"

I lean forward. "And what?"

"Nothing." She clears her throat. "I don't like being out there, but it's going to be fine for the show of it, right?"

I'm trying to read between the lines, and the best that I can come up with is that Mira doesn't *actually* snowboard. The more I think on it, though, slotting her into her family dynamics, the clearer the picture becomes.

They probably wouldn't even notice if she got all dressed up in the outfit, with the board, then slipped away before getting on the lift.

My chest tightens at the thought of my family treating me that way.

They'd never.

"Some slope action, some dinners. Anything else?"

She slowly shakes her head. "I don't want to take you away from your friends."

I snort. "They'll be fine if I'm a little absent. Now… about those orgasms?"

"Not happening," she says immediately. "No sex. We're building a wall of pillows between us."

I eye her. "Mira."

"What?"

"Your family won't believe that I'm your boyfriend if you don't kiss me."

"And—"

"*And* if you're not comfortable with me. Physically."

Her gaze skips around the room. "I'm fine."

"We'll discuss the orgasms at a later date," I decide. "But I require at *least* two public kisses. With tongue. Or the whole deal is off."

She glares at me, but I just smile. And after a beat, I hold out my hand for her to shake.

For a second, she has me convinced she's not going to take it.

But then her hand slides into mine, her cold fingers squeezing tightly, and my smile broadens.

"Let the games begin, Frostbite."

CHAPTER 6
MIRA

I'VE JUST FINISHED UNPACKING when Rhys walks through the door after eating dinner with his group of friends. I opted for one of the granola bars that I stuffed in my bag, knowing I'd skip out on as many family outings as I could.

Especially now that I have a fake boyfriend who my family will expect to accompany me.

What was I thinking?

My sisters' faces pop into my mind to remind me of exactly what I was thinking—or rather feeling.

Embarrassment.

To know that Rhys overheard them…*ugh*. My face bursts into flames again, even hours later.

"Did you leave me any space in there?" Rhys peers over my shoulder and into the dresser. "Oooh, I can't wait to see you in this."

Suddenly, my hot-pink bathing suit is dangling from his pinky finger while he grins at me. I've never seen a grin be so…hot.

I huff and snatch my suit out of his grasp. "Give me that!"

His chuckle is flirty at best.

I turn to hide the twitching of my lips because I have a feeling it'll only encourage him further. I scoot my things over in the drawer. "There." I nod to the room I made for him.

Rhys hums under his breath then turns and walks over to his suitcase. I'm surprised to see that it's nice and tidy, all his articles of clothing folded neatly. He grabs his stack of boxers and places them into the drawer beside my bathing suits and then moves to the bottom drawer to add the rest of his clothing.

I purposely put my panties and bras underneath my bathing suits, hopeful he won't see them. If he poked fun at my bathing suit, I'm not sure what he'll say when he sees my thongs.

"I'm heading to the hot tub," he says with my back to him.

I peer over my shoulder. "Oka—" My jaw falls. "Rhys!"

Wow, that's a nice backside.

"What?" He's so unbothered.

With a breath lodged in my throat, I quickly spin around. "Warn me next time! How has it only been a few hours, and I've seen you naked not once, but twice?"

"You know…" Rhys shuffles towards the back door. "I think it's only fair that I see you naked since you've seen me naked."

I huff sarcastically and glance at him. "It's not like I wanted to see you naked!"

Rhys shrugs while smiling widely to show off his perfectly straight teeth. "I think you did. You just don't want to admit it."

When the sliding door closes, I exhale.

Sharing a cabin with Rhys is going to be exhausting. He has the same amount of energy as he did when we were kids, except he's put that energy toward tormenting me with his witty remarks and teases instead of playing in the backyard for hours upon hours.

This was supposed to be a relaxing ski trip, aside from the

time spent with my family, and now it's turned into *this*: blocking flirty remarks from my old neighbor-friend and doting on him while in public.

My phone vibrates on the table for the fifteenth time since I saw my sisters in the lobby, and I choose to ignore it —*again*.

They're curious.

The news has spread.

My mom sent a text and asked why I didn't mention that my boyfriend was joining us, but I ignored that message, too, mainly because how do I explain that Rhys and I have been dating for all of three seconds?

I roll my eyes.

What did I get myself into?

My gaze skips over to the sliding door that Rhys disappeared through. I nibble on my lip from my frazzled nerves, and before I know it, I'm walking over and pushing back the drapes slightly.

My mouth runs dry the longer I stare at him. He sits in the hot tub, but his back is to the slopes. He faces the cabin, like he's waiting for me to come join him. Thankfully, his head is tipped backward, and his eyes are closed. The ripples of the jets send foamy bubbles up to this chest, but that doesn't distract me from dragging my gaze from each of his shoulders and bulging muscles.

Rhys is hot.

The idea of kissing him doesn't seem that bad all of a sudden.

Wait, no.

That's not a good idea.

My shoulders fall with the disappointment from my rational thinking.

It would be irrational to kiss him… or more. *Right*?

A knock sounds from the front door to the cabin, and I freeze.

If it isn't the girl from the lobby to tell me that she found me a new cabin, then I'm not answering.

Another knock echoes, and that's when my sister's high-pitched voice hits my ears.

"I swear, Marcus! You're going to owe me twenty bucks when you open this door and see that Mira really does have a boyfriend!"

Oh, fuck me.

I glance at the sliding door and make a last-minute decision.

Boyfriend and girlfriend, here we come.

CHAPTER 7
RHYS

IT'S PROBABLY stupid to pretend to be Mira's boyfriend. I don't date. Thorne has tried to cajole me into it, but the girls who surround me are all so fixated on football. They want to be the girlfriend of a football player. And if I make it pro, they want to be the *wife* of a football player.

That sort of mentality creates some trust issues.

Thorne and Aaron got lucky. Jack, too. Their girls are down-to-earth. Briar is a bit too grumpy for my taste, but whatever. Thorne eats up her bullshit with a silver spoon. I don't know the rest well enough to judge.

Mira, on the other hand…

Not grumpy.

Maybe a little sad? Frustrated, for some reason?

Seems like we'll have more than a week to dig into it, since we'll now be spending a decent amount of time together.

I went to dinner with my friends and couldn't even muster up the story. I opened my mouth to tell them about it —the strange chain of events that led to Mira becoming my fake girlfriend—but no words came out.

Like a switch flipping, I went from wanting to laugh about

it to feeling oddly protective. Mira doesn't deserve to be poked at, not when her family clearly does it so well.

There's a splash, and I open my eyes. Mira is climbing into the water, but—

"Why are you naked?" Familiar words. But this time they come from me. Directed at *her*.

"No time to explain." She practically falls into the water, submerging her body up to her shoulders. She throws herself in my direction. Her hands land on my shoulders.

I'm naked.

"Is this you taking me up on the orgasms offer?" *Damn*, my voice is hopeful.

"No. Shut up."

She scrambles against me, her smooth legs making contact with mine. She straddles my lap, and my hands automatically fall to her hips. My fingers find the strip of her panties, giving away that she's not *totally* naked. Barely. Just topless.

"So, um, play along." Her cheeks heat.

My eyebrows lift, and it takes everything in my power not to drop my gaze to her breasts. I don't want to peek and get hard and ruin what feels like a tentative, desperate move on her part. Except, I can't quite figure out *why* she's acting like this.

I keep my hands glued to her hips so they don't go wandering, seeing as how she doesn't actually seem to be into that right now.

Snow crunching nearby distracts me from her nipples.

Wait, maybe I should distract *her*.

"Kiss me." Her voice comes out hoarse and raspy.

Fuck me, my dick has entered the chat. I drag her closer to me, and she smashes her chest to mine. My hands finally release her hips and wander up, one splayed across her back, the other tracing the side of her ribs, to the outer swell of her breast. I cup her cheek and draw her in, just as the voices reach me.

"She might be hiding out back," a guy says. "We just need to bust her alone and then everyone can chill. She's the type to run after a lie. Remember when she backed into that fire hydrant and told Dad it was a hit-and-run? We didn't see her for a week."

Someone else snorts. "True. If that's the case, she might be in her cabin all week."

Assholes.

Mira sucks in a breath, but it doesn't matter. I pull her in and angle my head, pressing my lips to hers. For a second, neither of us move. Her nipples brush my chest, her thighs straddling mine—it all fades when her lips part. I take advantage, straightening up and sliding my fingers into her hair. I tilt her head with a tug and lick along her lower lip.

Just a taste.

My heart skips. Her fingers dig into my shoulders.

She deepens the kiss. Her tongue pushes into my mouth, and I groan. I wrap my arm around her back to make sure she can't escape the minute her siblings discover us. Because I'm sure they're about to round the corner and make some racket, and I don't want this to end.

Her tongue withdraws. I suck her lower lip between my teeth, scoring it, until a rumbling hum reverberates through her chest and into mine. There's a rushing sound in my ears.

Why is this kiss better than anything I've experienced?

I'd take this kiss over a blow job.

My cock is so fucking hard. It's trapped between our bodies, and she rolls her hips forward slightly. The friction of her wet panties on me is too much. I'm going to come just from that—and what an embarrassment that would be.

"Holy shit," one of Mira's sisters—*it has to be a stupid sister*—says. "I told you so!"

My grip tightens ever so slightly in Mira's hair, keeping her with me for another second.

"No one likes a know-it-all," the guy grumbles.

Mira pulls back, and I open my eyes as soon as possible to catch the dazed expression in her eyes. But just as fast, it's gone, and annoyance is in its place. Her head whips to the side.

Mine follows.

Her siblings stand there in shock. Belatedly, I move to cover Mira's chest. Just because they're family doesn't mean I want *them* to see her breasts. I'm laying claim on them as of this instant.

Fake dating or not, that kiss was a sucker punch I wasn't prepared for.

"Cammie," Mira says, somehow calm. "Marcus. What are you doing?"

Marcus is a tall kid, and he's currently staring at *me*. Which is probably better than eyeing Mira, but still. He's wide-eyed, but after a second, he elbows his sister. His movements are urgent, and I barely withhold my smirk. He seems *flabbergasted*. And I don't think it's because some guy is with Mira. It's because *I* am with Mira.

"We were just coming to check on you," Cammie blurts out. "Because you guys missed dinner."

Mira clenches her jaw.

I went to dinner with my friends—so, did Mira do nothing?

I run my hand down her spine, trying to tell her without words to relax, and direct my words at Cammie.

"We got a little distracted. Hope you all didn't wait too long for us." I focus on Mira. "She's just irresistible."

"I feel like I'm in *The Twilight Zone*," Cammie whispers.

I clear my throat. "If you don't mind, you're kind of cock blocking right now. We'll catch up with you all tomorrow."

I make a *shoo*ing motion.

Marcus pales.

Cammie turns red, worse than a tomato. She grabs

Marcus's arm and practically drags him back the way they came.

Once they're gone, Mira shoves off my lap. Her expression shows she's horrified, and she wastes no time climbing out of the hot tub. I shake my head, somehow holding in my laughter. My family is so… *normal* compared to those assholes. And honestly, there's nothing I like better than messing with jerks —which means this week just got a whole lot more interesting.

I follow Mira into the cabin. She chucks a towel at me, which I dutifully use to rub myself down enough to not drip water across the floor on my way to the bathroom. I shower fast and trade with Mira. From the top drawer in the dresser, I pull out a fresh pair of boxers.

My hands still when I notice her underwear tucked under the bikini she didn't put on.

Honestly, a naked-hot-tub session trumps a swimsuit, so I don't mind. The water is still running in the bathroom, so I take my chances and push aside the hot-pink fabric.

Aha! She wears full coverage panties in various plain, neutral colors. I run my thumb across the waistband of one, considering.

Mira's family seems to think she's a loner or a prude. I haven't figured out which one. *But* I'd lean toward loner simply because of the balls it took to get into the hot tub shirtless.

I smile to myself. The panties kind of contradict that, but whatever. It's not like I'm walking around in form-fitting briefs. I bet thongs are uncomfortable, especially since she thought she'd be rooming alone.

Wait.

I dig deeper into the drawer, my attention hooking on a bit of red lace.

Naughty girl.

I lift it out, and my brows furrow. How the fuck does this

go on? It's *all* lace, with absolutely zero structure. No cups for breasts...

Shit.

I swallow hard, my dick once again waking up. It was a close call earlier, and I should've jacked off in the shower. Missed opportunity.

The door opens, and I'm caught red-handed. Her gaze on my back *burns*, and I slowly rotate toward her with the lingerie in my grip.

"Were you snooping?"

My face heats. "No. Yes. Maybe."

She scowls and marches forward. She's in an oversized t-shirt and leggings, her normally light-blonde hair darker now that it's wet. It's combed out, the locks loose around her shoulders. The feel of the soft strands comes to mind. She snatches the lace from me and stuffs it back into the drawer. She slams it shut.

"The question is..." I prop my elbow on the dresser. "Were you planning on seducing someone this week? A Christmas fling?"

Oh, her expression is priceless. And because I can't resist, I press further.

"Brave Mira, were you going to have a random holiday hookup?" I spread my arms. "Because, baby, I am totally available for the job."

She finally cracks, a smirk curving her plump lips. It makes me want to kiss her again, harder, so they get all puffy, and her family will have absolutely no illusions about what we did all night.

"I'm not going to take you up on that," she finally says.

Boo.

"And I want the side of the bed closest to the wall just in case someone breaks in and tries to kill us," she adds.

I blink, but Mira just moves around me. She goes to the far side of the bed and pulls down the blankets. She takes the decorative pillows and stuffs them under the blankets, making a line—no, a *wall*—down the center of the bed.

I raise my eyebrows.

"You stay on your side." She climbs in and gets comfortable. She watches me for a moment, probably because I'm still standing there like an idiot. "I mean it, Rhys."

"Got it. No touchie."

Seeing her in bed is hot.

I need to take care of my issue before I join her. By *issue*, I mean boner that is currently about to make an untimely appearance. If I don't, I'll fall asleep, and no number of pillows would keep me from gravitating toward her while unconscious.

CHAPTER 8
MIRA

DESPITE SHARING A BED WITH RHYS, I actually slept like a baby.

That's not to say I didn't have an extremely inappropriate dream that had to do with a hot tub, but I keep that information to myself because my fake boyfriend is *not* privy to knowing just how turned on I was after our impromptu kiss.

Kiss?

More like sex.

I was a disoriented afterward. My vision was hazy, and even though I opted for a cold shower, I was still sweating afterward.

Rhys can *kiss.*

"Okay, so fill me in on your fam. Give me all the tea." Rhys steeples his fingers together and taps them excitedly.

Is he eager for breakfast with my family? Because I'd rather take the lift up to the highest peak and attempt to ski it instead of playing twenty questions regarding our fake relationship over pancakes and coffee.

"We don't have enough time for that," I say.

The walk to the restaurant is less than five minutes. It'd

take five hours to name everyone and explain the moving parts of our blended family.

"Going in blind," he says. "I like your bravery, Mira."

I laugh sarcastically. "That's the only way to be when you're walking into a war zone."

Suddenly, Rhys's arm falls to my shoulders, and he pulls me in close. My body comes to life, which is a rare occurrence without any caffeine. "Don't worry. Your secret weapon is here, Frostbite."

From my shorter frame, I glare up at him. He winks when he catches my scowl, and *damn him.* My lips twitch, and I break into a smile. "You're irritating."

"That's no way to treat your boyfriend," he muses.

He pokes the side of my belly. A high-pitched laugh rushes from my mouth at the same time I try to escape his grip. Except, the ground is slick with ice, and I nearly bust my face.

Rhys's arm wraps around my waist, and we're suddenly flush. We're both wearing coats, but I swear the ridges of his toned muscles are pressing against me.

Last night totally messed with my head.

He grabs my chin. "Be careful, Mira."

A tight breath whooshes from my lungs.

His warm eyes shift back and forth between mine, and there's a protectiveness to his tone that seems awfully real. I glance around to see if my family is nearby, but we're surrounded by random resort guests who are paying us no attention.

"You can let me go now," I say. "I'm fine."

Rhys shoots me his golden-boy smile. "I know. I was just deciding if I should kiss you or not. You know… for practice."

My heart stalls.

The idea of him kissing me isn't as off-putting as it was yesterday.

"Mira!" Cammie's voice grates my nerves like no other. She *would* interrupt this.

"*Damn,*" Rhys mutters, letting me go.

He sends me a look that says he'll resume this later, but I'm pretty sure that's just my raging hormones talking.

"We were afraid you'd skip out on breakfast like you did with dinner."

Oh, trust me. I tried. Rhys wouldn't let me. He went on and on about how I didn't eat dinner last night and how he wasn't going to let me skip another meal.

It was sort of cute, but irritating.

"Figured we'd better make an appearance, or you'd come searching for us again." Rhys intertwines our fingers and guides me toward the restaurant, not really caring to see if my sister follows.

Unfortunately, she does.

"I got enough of an eyeful yesterday," she jokes.

She elbows me and wiggles her eyebrows when Rhys isn't paying attention. I roll my eyes. I know what she's getting at. She's in disbelief that Rhys is my boyfriend. I can't really blame her, though. He's *way* out of my league.

As soon as we enter the restaurant, I drag Rhys toward the back. From the loud laughter, a wailing cry from my nephew, and nails-on-a-chalkboard voice from Rachel as she scolds my brother-in-law for something, I know exactly where to go.

Cammie rushes in front of us and takes her seat, making way for the entire family to pause what they're doing when they see us. Rhys squeezes my hand, and it's the reassurance that I need to keep pushing forward.

"Good morning," I say.

Dragging my attention from the gaping mouths of ninety percent of my family, I hunt for two open seats.

Surprise, surprise.

There are none.

"Oh, seems like there isn't room for us! We will catch you

all later." I try to turn away with Rhys's hand in mine, but he grips it tightly and clears his throat.

"May we borrow two chairs?" he asks a couple sitting close by.

The woman stands eagerly. "Take all of them." Then she grabs her husband by the hand and finds a different table, halfway across the restaurant, away from the chaos.

I don't blame her, but she's totally losing out on free entertainment.

"Problem solved." Rhys winks at me while pushing two chairs up to the end of the table.

I begrudgingly move to pull my chair out, but he scolds me under his breath. "Absolutely not."

His eyebrow flicks upward in some sort of challenge. My cheeks warm, and I take a seat.

Cammie clears her throat. "Well…"

I lock onto her from across the table and refrain from throwing a fork at her head.

"Are you going to introduce your *boyfriend*?"

"Everyone, this is Rhys."

My family mutters a hello in sync, except for Liam, who is too busy screaming at the top of his lungs.

I resonate with him because I, too, would like to scream at the top of my lungs.

Rhys leans across the table and puts his hand out for my father to shake. "It's nice to see you again, sir."

"Again?" Marcus, who can't even look me in the eye after yesterday, seems suspicious.

"Ah, that's right." My dad squints. "You used to be our neighbor."

A murmur travels across the table.

I reach for the coffee, as if I'm not jittery enough.

My leg bounces while my dad and Rhys reminisce about the past. My mom and stepparents join in the conversation, too, but I remain quiet. Rachel and Cammie are talking quietly to themselves while glancing at Rhys and me every few seconds.

I try to kick them under the table, but my leg doesn't reach.

Rhys, who must notice my movement, places a hand on my knee and gives it a gentle squeeze, all while carrying on the conversation.

They ask him about his parents and school and nearly fall out of their chairs when he mentions the pros.

Marcus sits up straighter, forgetting all about my sister's gossip over my new relationship.

After we've given our orders and the conversation dies down—along with my nerves, thanks to Rhys's comforting rubbing against my knee—Cammie places her elbows on the table and rests her chin in the palms of her hands.

"Are you a skier, Rhys?"

Rhys leans back in his chair, giving a full view of how his hand is on my thigh under the table. "I've skied, but snowboarding is more my thing."

Cammie immediately flicks her amused gaze to me. "Mira, too. She always chooses to snowboard when we go skiing." Cammie twirls her hair in her finger. "Actually, we've never even seen her snowboard. For all we know, she hides out in the cabin, pretending to hit the slopes."

Rhys's hand travels up my thigh, and I'm sure he's trying to distract me, but sadly, nothing can distract me from my sister's annoying laugh.

"That's not true," I argue. "You're just too busy dry-humping Andrew to know what's going on around you."

"Mira," my mom warns.

Rhys's hand clamps onto my leg, and he clears his throat. I'm pretty sure it's to hide his laugh.

"Okay, fine." Cammie leans forward with a fake smile, and I know she's baiting me. "Andrew and I will come with you and your boyfriend to Bear's Peak, then."

"Bear's Peak?" Rhys repeats. "That's the highest—"

"We meet at ten." I raise an eyebrow at my sister, and pride swells in my chest.

Unfortunately, that pride disappears as soon as I realize that I've just signed my own death warrant.

I've never snowboarded in my life.

CHAPTER 9
RHYS

MIRA HAS NEVER SNOWBOARDED in her life, but she sure is sexy as hell trying.

After breakfast, which went a lot better than I was expecting, we parted ways to get dressed. My lovely fake girlfriend kept her mouth shut while we suited up. First, it was the leggings that clung to her thighs and ass. Then the *shimmy* she did to get those white snow pants up over her hips. She paired it with a matching white jacket and helmet and rainbow, mirrored goggles.

It really goes with her ice queen vibe—the pale skin, light-blonde hair, blue eyes. Of course, those features are all now safely hidden away, protected from the cold wind that'll soon assault us.

It went downhill once we grabbed our boards and headed out.

First, she tried to clip into her board backward, which didn't even make sense. The bindings are kind of self-explanatory. I had a good chuckle about that, and it earned me one of her pretty glares.

Once that was sorted, she inched toward the lift in some sort of wiggle, both boots clipped in, and her eyebrows hiked when I tugged her to a stop. Luckily, no one saw her. Probably. The line was already long, and we were immediately separated from Cammie and Andrew. *Unfortunately*, they ended up behind us, so there was no chance of Mira and me ducking away.

"You've been on a lift before, right?"

I collect another glare for my collection, filed under *If Looks Could Kill*. Damn. I hold up my hands in surrender, hoping for a smile.

Or a smirk.

I'd settle for a rueful headshake at this point.

Nada.

And then, suddenly, we're next up. This lift is fancy, which means shuffling forward when the attendant motions, facing the mountain, and letting the chair come up behind us to sweep us away.

Mira lets out a squeak when the bar hits the backs of her knees. I grab her gloved hand, and once our feet have left the ground, I reach up with my free hand and lower the bar in front of us. She slips her hand from mine and grips the bar hard.

"Mira."

She shakes her head.

My brows furrow, and I lean closer. "Are you okay?"

Her lips press into a thin line. "I'm totally fine."

Oh, boy. It's worse than I thought.

I crane around, and the chair swings a bit. Mira makes a choking noise, but I temporarily ignore it in the attempt to spot her sister and brother-in-law. Her whole family is irritating, but judging by Mira's complete and utter lack of snowboarding knowledge, she's never been *on the slopes*. Even though they apparently do this sort of holiday every winter. Even though she literally grew up around these people.

I can't see much beyond the two behind us, and neither one appears to hold Cammie and what's-his-face. When I turn back around, Mira's goggles are off, and her eyes are squeezed shut tight. Her whole face is scrunched.

"Oh, fuck." It dawns on me. "You're afraid of heights."

"Nope," she squeaks.

"Liar." I scoot closer, causing our chair to bounce. I haul her toward me, into the center of the long chair. And it's *fine*, because suddenly we're pressed together from hip to knee.

Her knee anyway, since she's a lot shorter.

I wrap my arm around her shoulders, and with my other hand, I bring her face toward my chest. "Breathe with me, and I'll tell you when you can look."

Her body trembles slightly, but she does what I say. I exaggerate the rise and fall of my chest, sucking in deep breaths for her to mimic. When she does, satisfaction—and a thread of worry—fills my chest. I rub her arm and lift my gaze away from the top of her helmet to scope out the run beneath us. It's a black diamond, and we're passing a section of moguls. It's probably for the best that she doesn't see this portion. No need to freak her out more.

Step one: get her safely off the lift.

Step two: figure out how to get her down the mountain without killing both of us...or further damaging her reputation with her family.

I know why she rose to the challenge set out by her sister. It seems like the whole family is hell-bent on antagonizing her —or ignoring her.

My parents would *never*. Sure, my mom often kicked me out of the house as a kid, but that was because I was an insufferable ball of energy and she worked from home. When we were home from school or off for the summer, she got the short end of the stick.

Luckily, we all survived, and my relationship with my parents is solid. It's why they're sad I'm not going to be home for Christmas, even if they understood the need for this trip. I *am* going pro. I will get drafted, and my life will be a whole lot different in a few years.

Hell, a few *months*.

When we were planning this trip, piled around the living room in November, exhausted from midterms, hope bubbled through me. My friends were right in front of my face, but I missed them, nonetheless.

Now, locked into this ruse with Mira, I'm still not getting my fill of them. But how would they react if I showed up with her in tow? I can't lie to them. It took everything in me to not blurt it out at dinner last night when they asked how my hot tub was treating me.

Ugh.

"Okay," I eventually say. "We're going to have to get off in a minute. I want you to copy me, all right?"

Her head bobbles against my chest with her nod.

"Wait just a second, we're still a bit high. Then you can open your eyes." I take a deep breath. "Then we're gonna put this bar up, scootch to the edge of the seat kind of at an angle so when the ramp comes, we can hop off and slide down."

This isn't going to be pretty.

"I'll help you. Okay?"

"Yeah," she manages.

The lift descends, and I tell her when it's okay to open her eyes. She raises her head and blinks, meeting my gaze then quickly glancing around.

"Got it. This is totally fine." She clears her throat.

The bar comes up, and we shift.

"Put your back foot in front of the binding." I put my hand on her hip. "Yep, just like that."

We watch the people on the chair in front of us, but they're both skiers. Then it's our turn. Together, we hop off. I grab her waist, keeping her steady on the short ramp. She's way too stiff, her whole body locked up, but I navigate us away from some clusters of people to a quiet, flatter spot.

"That was good." I focus on her face. "There are only blue and black runs up here. Blue will be our best bet, but we have a minute. Probably need to show our faces to your sister."

Her cheeks are flushed, but she grimaces and nods. She slowly lowers the goggles back into place, shielding her eyes from view.

Not a moment too soon, because her evil sister gets off the lift a second later. I face Mira again then kneel to help get her foot in the binding.

I shouldn't say evil. That's cruel.

What I *should* call her is self-centered, spoiled, no-good—

"Rhys?"

I jerk. "Sorry. What?"

My hands are on her calf and boot, and I think I might've just been frozen there.

"I said, I'm sorry—"

I shake it off and finish getting her binding secured. "No. Don't do that."

I rise.

And then Cammie and the brother-in-law are in front of us, both smiling widely.

"We thought we lost you!" she coos. "That would've been a shame. We were eyeing the slope under the lift. It looked really fun. What do you think, Mira?"

My fake girlfriend squares her shoulders, suddenly smiling broadly.

Cammie is talking about the trail with the moguls—the one that is probably a double black diamond.

The one that we should avoid at all costs.

"Sounds great."

Nope.

Bad.

Bad, bad, bad.

"Great!" Cammie's husband says. "It's decided."

"No," I blurt out.

They all pause.

Shit.

"I, um… I can't do that one, guys. I had a health scare with an old knee injury"—*Thank you, Thorne, for never shutting up about yours*—"and all those moguls might aggravate it. It's rehabbed, but with my future at stake…"

"Oh my God, Rhys, you're so right." Mira smacks my chest. "I'm sorry. We should pick something a little less… extreme."

"Blue is more my speed these days," I say.

Cammie and her husband, whose name I should really clarify, shift and nod.

"If you guys want to go for the other one, we can just meet you at the bottom."

"Oh, yeah, good idea," the husband says.

"If you can make it down in one piece, Mira." Cammie smirks. "I've got to say, I'm surprised you even made it up here. Last one down is a rotten egg?"

We manage nods, and then they're gone.

I blow out a breath.

One problem conquered. I don't even mind being labeled a rotten egg.

The next is getting Mira down in one piece.

CHAPTER 10
MIRA

IT WAS my idea to pretend I had a boyfriend, and it was my idea to pretend I knew how to snowboard.

I am zero for two at this point.

"Shit!" I bury my face in my hands, as if hiding from the situation is going to make things better.

Rhys grabs on to my wrists with his gloved hands and lowers them. It's hard to know what he's thinking, because his eyes are hidden behind his goggles, but when his lip lifts into a smirk, I find myself taking a much-needed breath.

"We make a good team, Frostbite."

"A good team?!" I shriek. "I'm going to die. I can't snow-board, Rhys!"

Rhys's smirk turns into a full-on smile. Butterflies swarm my stomach, and it surprises me so much that I don't even notice that he's taken my hands in his and is pulling me to a flatter area.

"Do you trust me?" he asks.

Yes.

Wait, do I?

"Mira." Rhys squeezes my hands.

"Yeah," I answer. "I suppose."

"I won't let you die." He positions me where he wants me. "Not until after I kiss you a few more times."

I open my mouth to argue, but he shuts me up real quick by letting go of me. I'm on even ground, but without him helping me, I panic. A shriek works up my throat when I start sliding down the slope, but I'm quickly stopped when Rhys's hands slip to my waist.

"Jeez," he mutters. "Worse than I thought."

"I told you!" I argue. "Never mind that I'm going to die going down this slope"—I push my goggles up to get a better look at it—"but Cammie will never let me live it down when I lose."

"You care that much about beating her down the mountain?"

I nod vehemently.

Rhys does the same to his goggles, revealing a furrowed brow with determination. "Okay, Frostbite. We are *not* going to lose."

His panty-dropping smirk reappears, and anticipation fills me…until he kneels in front of me and unstraps my feet from the snowboard.

"What are you doing?" I step back onto the packed snow.

"You mean, what are *we* doing?" He holds out my board for me to take. Once it's in my possession, he takes my goggles and slides them back to their rightful spot. Then he moves to my coat and makes sure it's zipped all the way before sliding along the snow to put his back to me. "Get on, Spider Monkey."

I freeze. "What?"

"Get on my back, Mira. I'll get us to the bottom."

He taps his shoulder, and I stare at the back of him like he is insane.

"You cannot give me a piggy-back ride all the way down the slope!"

Rhys bends down so I can climb on, as if he doesn't care

about my argument. "We'll take a break halfway. Hurry up, or we're going to lose, and then I'll have to get ugly with your sister when she pokes fun at you."

I weigh my options. Which is better? Beating Cammie or hearing my fake boyfriend put her in her place? Both are good, if you ask me.

"Mira."

I sigh. "Fine!"

While holding my board with a tight grip, I climb onto Rhys. I wrap my legs around his waist, and I manage to trap my board between my chest and his back while securing myself around his neck.

"Good girl," he whispers, smiling at me over his shoulder.

"I'm not a dog!" I snap.

Rhys's shoulders shake with laughter. "My fake girlfriend doesn't like to be called a good girl. Got it."

My cheeks flush, and I thank my lucky stars that he can't see them.

Before we take off down the slope, Rhys peers back at me once more. "I bet you like to be called a good girl in bed, though."

My stomach flips, and I clamp my legs tighter around him. His rough chuckle is left behind as he takes off snow-boarding with me hanging on to him for dear life.

It doesn't take long for me to start to slip. Every couple of minutes, Rhys hoists me up higher onto his back, and I press into him in fear that I'll fall backward and be stranded in the snow until I die of hypothermia.

Rhys tilts forward a little, and I press harder into him. He mumbles something, but I can't hear him from the speed and wind. When I see a little clearing off to the side near a bundle of trees, I flex my hips a few times to get his attention.

He reads my sign well, heading to our break point.

As soon as he stops, I try to jump down to relieve his back, but his gloved hands hold me hostage against him.

"Don't do that," he warns.

I lift my goggles to get a better read on him. "Do what?"

"Hump me."

A burst of laughter flies from my mouth. "What?"

"Just a second ago. You humped me. *Twice.*" Rhys's tongue slips out of his mouth, and he wets his bottom lip.

I stare at it for a brief second before attempting to wiggle out of his grip.

Rhys flips his goggles up and then firmly places his hand back to my calf to keep me in place. "Are you trying to get fucked in the snow?"

A dirty thought enters my mind, and I'm blaming it on the sultry glint in his eye versus the amused, flirty one he's been giving me since ending up as his roommate.

I wiggle again, trying to slide down.

Rhys's gaze flickers with something *hot.*

This is a terrible idea.

We're definitely going to lose now if we fool around halfway down the slope.

"Oh, look," Rhys muses. "Your sister."

I attempt to turn and glance behind me, but before I know it, Rhys has me flat on my back in the snow. One of his knees shimmies in between mine, and even through all of our snow gear, I feel the heat coming off him in waves.

"You've worked up a sweat from carrying me." I sort of feel bad. "I'm sorry."

"Don't apologize." His mouth twitches with humor. "But now it's your turn to work up a sweat."

Rhys's glove slips from his hand and falls beside my head. He slowly creeps his fingers underneath my layers, and I've forgotten all about the race with my annoying sister.

The light brushing of Rhys's warm fingers against my stomach sends a flutter of pleasure between my legs. When he dips his finger beneath the waistband of my snowpants, our eyes catch.

Is he asking for my permission?

Because if so, he has it.

I grin and open my legs a little wider. I may not make it down the slope before Cammie, but I have a feeling my win is going to be better than hers.

CHAPTER 11
RHYS

I'M LIVING in an alternate reality.

One where my old crush, my old neighbor, is under me in the snow and letting me put my hand down her pants like we're in high school. This feels *forbidden*. And dangerous.

And like everything I never knew I wanted, all bundled into a white ski outfit.

I angle my body to keep what I'm doing from view. I dig my hand deeper, my fingers seeking the edge of her panties. The smooth—*damn, Mira, you're smooth down here?*—skin drawing me lower. Until I meet her arousal, and my heart damn near skips a beat.

She's wet.

Fuck me twice, my dick rises to the occasion, even though this is *not* the time or place for that. She'd get frostbite on her ass, and then the nickname really would be ironic.

"Touch me," Mira breathes.

I oblige. And, listen, I'm not gonna lie. I have some experience in this department. Not with Mira, of course, but other girls. The ones who tend to seek me out at parties or on campus…

Why the fuck am I thinking about them?

I focus on the feel. My fingers memorize the landscape of her pussy, and I slowly push one finger inside her.

"Ah, fuck," she groans. Her eyelashes flutter.

"When's the last time you were fucked?"

Her gaze flies to my face.

I add a finger, pumping into her with as much movement as her clothing allows. I grind the heel of my palm against her clit, and her mouth opens.

"When?" I grit out.

"I don't know." Her hips move. "A while ago, probably."

"Probably?" I smirk. "Then I should *probably* stop so you can think straight."

"Oh my God." She grabs my forearm. "Don't you dare."

Behind us, a new wave of skiers and snowboarders comes down the mountain. Their shouts float over us, and Mira's muscles clamp around my fingers.

"A little exhibitionist, hmm?" I lean down before she can answer, pressing my lips to hers. I increase my hand movement, my brain warring between leaving her hanging until later and wanting to feel her orgasm right this minute.

Her grip on my arm tenses. I keep the pressure up while my lips drift against hers. Her face is cold, but her mouth opens up for me. And when she sucks my tongue into her mouth, my dick pulses.

Fucking hell, she's not even touching me, and *I'm* ready to burst.

I shift my weight, seeking relief. When her palm comes down over my groin, I pause.

Hold it together.

We're in public.

And yet, thinking of my grandma or something embarrassing that happened when I was a kid doesn't hold a candle to how Mira occupies my mind. And my hand. We probably appear obscene, and maybe I have an exhibitionist kink, too, because only a few over-the-pants strokes of her hand has me coming in my pants.

I kiss her harder, the pleasure rushing from my balls, tingling up my spine. Hopefully she didn't realize... *Must distract.* I increase pressure, tempo, and her hand falls away from my pants as she comes.

I swallow her cries, and only when she goes limp do I ease back.

My gaze drops to my lap, and thank *fuck* I'm wearing black snow pants, plus athletic shorts, plus my briefs. The layers will hopefully hold my cover until I can get back to the cabin and change.

"Good girl," I say, just to see if it'll piss her off.

Her face flushes, and she hurriedly pulls her goggles back down.

I laugh and shake my head then push myself to my feet. I hold out my hands, which Mira takes after a split second of hesitation. She steps away from me and straightens her jacket and pants and finds where her board ended up.

I lower my goggles and pick up my forgotten gloves, sparing a moment to lick my fingers before sliding them back into the warmth.

Not the *right* warmth, but it'll do.

"Let's get down this mountain." I smirk. "And we'll see if you continue humping me."

———

"There you are!" Briar's voice rings out, stopping me in my tracks.

Oops.

I pivot, my arms laden with snowboarding gear. Thorne and Briar make their way up toward my cabin. They're wearing matching knit hats with ridiculous, oversized pom-

poms on top. Thorne's is mainly red with threads of green, while Briar's is the opposite.

God, Mira better not make me wear something like that.

"You two are ridiculous."

Briar scowls at me. She's been happier with Thorne—versus the prickly version of herself she *used* to be—but she still knows how to send a classic withering look.

"You've been MIA," Thorne says. He hops up the porch steps and gestures for my key.

I freeze.

"What?"

"It's a mess in there," I blurt out. I set my stuff down on the porch. "You guys hungry?"

"You're not even going to put your gear inside?" Thorne narrows his eyes. "What on earth is wrong with you?"

Oh, just the fact that there's an extra suitcase and *girl shit* spread across the cabin. We've been here one night—*one night*—and it's like a bomb went off. I literally saw her unpack her stuff into the dresser, but it doesn't matter. Overnight, someone must've come to terrorize us by sprinkling her items around every surface.

Something tells me it's only going to get worse.

"They're doing a tree-lighting thing tonight," Briar says. "We're all gonna go after dinner. They advertised live music and hot cocoa."

"Yeah? That sounds fun." I hastily unlock the door and shove my stuff in then pause.

I came in my briefs like an *idiot* earlier, and I can't very well go wandering back to the lodge for lunch wearing my ski boots.

I point at them. "Stay. Two seconds."

Before they can reply, I lock myself in and lock them out. It takes a minute to get out of the boots, then another to shuck the rest of my lower-half layers. I rush to the bathroom and use a washcloth to clean the waistband of my pants, which collected my mess, and grimace.

Did Mira notice?

Is *that* why she suddenly seemed more embarrassed?

Of course I'm going to ruin whatever this is. Fake or not, we were getting along. I mean, I wasn't kissing and fingering her for the hell of it.

Okay, I was. But there's also an attraction to her that I'm not going to deny. It lives *right there*, under my skin, and when she's around, I can't ignore it.

Her.

I can't ignore *her*.

One of my friends bangs on the door.

I pull on fresh boxers and jeans, socks, and my winter boots. They're both exasperated by the time I re-emerge.

"Finally," Thorne mutters. "Would've been nice for you to invite us in."

"But then you would've seen all my sex toys." I frown. "Some things are meant to stay private."

Briar chokes on her laugh. "TMI, Anderson. No one needs to know what you get up to at night."

I snicker. "Sure thing, B."

"Back to the conversation we were in the middle of… You're going to join us tonight? It's Christmas, after all."

"Well, it's not quite Christmas," I hedge. "We've got three more days."

Guilt worms through me that I'm not celebrating with my family. I sent their presents home before we left, so the giant box of wrapped goodies should be arriving any day now.

"Plus," I add, "you guys are too busy fucking to notice my absence."

Briar turns red.

Gotcha.

"Okay, okay." Thorne shakes his head. "You hungry? We

were gonna meet up with everyone and grab lunch then either hit the slopes or do the music bingo thing."

"Music bingo? Are we on vacation at an assisted living facility?" I grimace. "I'm starved, but I'm not playing music bingo unless it's *strip* music bingo."

Their easy laughter is a welcome change from Mira's uptight family.

"But you already went snowboarding?"

I focus on Briar as I herd them off my porch and back up the road toward the main lodge. "Um, yeah, early bird gets the worm or whatever. I was eager to test out the new board. It's great, by the way. Thanks for asking."

"I told you he was going to be lonely," Briar mutters, elbowing her boyfriend.

Thorne shoots her a look.

"I'm not lonely." I roll my eyes. "I've been finding plenty of entertainment."

Simultaneously, their attention swings back to me. My statement might've sounded a little dirty, sure, but they're the ones whose minds are in the gutter.

I scratch my jaw. "I mean, uh—"

"Oh my God, you found a hookup already?" Briar laughs.

A flush works its way up my neck, accosting my cheeks. Because my traitorous brain goes right back to the mischief Mira and I got up to on the slopes this morning…

Sure, we made it down in one piece, and we didn't even run into Mira's sister or brother-in-law. We *did* see her parents, who looked ready to head toward the lift. They invited us, and before I could make up a lie, Mira blurted out something about the binding on her board needing to be fixed.

Once gone, we split up. Me to drop off mine, Mira to pretend to get her board repaired for appearances' sake. Or something. I don't know—maybe she just wanted to be free from me after that orgasm. It was spontaneous and a bit stupid, a definite risk to both of our reputations if we had been caught…

My insides haven't been so twisted up since my first college game as a starter.

"Don't listen to her, Rhys." Thorne pats my back. "You can hook up with whomever you want."

Briar shakes her head. She beats us both to the door, yanking it open and sweeping her arm to usher us in.

"That's my job, kitten," Thorne rumbles. He pauses at her elbow, his hand going to the side of her face. He leans down—

Gag.

I miss their kiss, instead bypassing them and slipping into the warm lodge. Across the lobby, past the reception desk, I spot the rest of our friends standing at the hostess stand.

I take a breath and continue forward. Hopefully Mira's family is nowhere near this restaurant, because I'm not sure how I'd explain this group to them. Or vice versa.

CHAPTER 12
MIRA

I DECIDE to give Rhys the night off, feeding an excuse to my family that he's on a video call with his family while they open his gifts. Meanwhile, I'm forced on a nonnegotiable family outing to the tree lighting in the center of the resort.

The pine tree stands tall in the courtyard behind the lodge, the tip of it so high I have to crane my neck to see the bright star. Liam, with his rosy-red cheeks, is on top of my dad's shoulders to see better. Marcus acts like a child and secretly throws snowballs at the back of my sister's head to piss her off.

I laugh under my breath every time the powder explodes against her coat.

Until he hits me.

"Marcus." I spin with gritted teeth. "Don't play with me. You know I'll get you back."

Cold snow slides down my neck and underneath the back of my sweater. A chill works through me, and I can't help but bend down to make my own snowball.

"I would be afraid if your boyfriend was here." Marcus chuckles. "But he's not. Did he break up with you already?"

I roll my eyes, all while packing my snowball tighter. "If he did, it'd be because of how crazy my family is."

Marcus makes the mistake of taking his eyes from me.

I palm the snowball a few times until passersby move out of the way. When the coast is clear, I wind my arm back and send it flying. It smacks him on the side of his head, and my laughter erupts.

"Mira!" my mom scolds me, but I truly couldn't care less.

Maybe it's the random orgasm that Rhys gave me, or maybe it's just Rhys's presence in general. Either way, I'm much more chipper today than I've ever been while on a family trip.

I fake an apology to my mom and turn away from my brother. There's a weird pang in my stomach that comes with the thought of Rhys.

Do I miss him?

No. Surely not.

It would be insane to miss my fake boyfriend, right? And it's not like he's *gone*. He's just taking a break from being forced to do *my* stuff.

"Hey, Mira… isn't that your boyfriend?" My brother's tone is laced with amusement.

But I'm not stupid enough to fall for his tricks.

"Nice try, Marcus," I call over my shoulder. "I know the second I turn around, you're going to hit me dead center in the face with a snowball."

"Boy…fwiend!" Liam claps his hands while my dad holds him steady on his shoulders.

Butterflies fill my stomach, and warmth rushes in. *Why did I just get butterflies?*

I follow Liam's line of sight, forgetting all about Marcus and our snowball fight, and spin over the slippery ground.

"Think fast!" Marcus shouts.

My hands fly up to block the hit, but nothing comes. Someone grabs my wrists and slowly pulls my face free.

I blink several times before snapping out of my trance. Rhys stands in front of me with the hottest smirk I've ever seen.

"Need some backup, Frostbite?"

Excitement forces a real smile onto my face. Rhys jerks slightly at the sight of it.

"You should smile more often," he whispers. "It's a pretty one."

A knot forms in my throat from the compliment. Does he mean that? Or is he just playing along with the whole boyfriend thing?

"Bro, I'm sorry. I didn't mean to hit you."

Rhys drops my wrists and wraps his arm around my waist. "I know. You were trying to hit my girl."

My cheeks burst with heat. *His girl.*

Marcus shrugs sheepishly. "She started it."

I gasp. "I did not."

Rhys chuckles and peers down at me. "Want to go get some hot cocoa?"

"Hot cocoa!" Liam chants from behind me.

I wrinkle my nose at him. "Do you want some hot cocoa, too?"

My dad grabs his wallet and offers me money. "Hurry before your sister sees and tells us he can't have sugar."

I laugh and reach forward for the money, but Rhys quickly tugs me backward. "I've got it. Anyone else want some?"

Marcus pipes up. "Me."

Rhys glances at him. "Only if you stop throwing snow-balls at my girlfriend."

"Done."

I roll my eyes at my brother before heading towards the hot cocoa stand. Once we're out of earshot, I peek at him. "What are you doing here? I gave you the night off."

Rhys blows air out of his puffed-up cheeks. "We've got a problem, Frostbite."

Panic forces me to stop walking. "You want to break up?"

Shit.

My heart jolts, and I fear it's the beginning of an upcoming heartbreak from my fake boyfriend breaking up with me, which means I'm more delusional than I thought.

"Okay," I start babbling. "We will need a plan. Maybe make a scene? We can get into a big fight." My teeth sink into my lip as I think of reasons for our fight. "Maybe you can say that you don't want a commitment—"

Rhys grips my chin, his hold firm but steady.

Silence takes over.

His thumb frees my lip from my teeth, and his eyes shift back and forth between mine. "I don't want to break up. We haven't even had sex yet."

He's joking.

I think.

He gently skims his thumb against my lip. "I expected a refusal or, at the very least, a scoff." His eyebrow rises beneath his beanie. "Interesting."

The snow under my boots makes a noise with my shifting. I wouldn't be surprised if it started to melt from the heat brewing between my legs at the thought of having sex with Rhys.

I clear my throat. "No breakup, then. What's the problem?"

Rhys glances back and forth. "You know how I came here with my friends? Well, they're starting to notice my more-than-usual absence, and Briar brought up coming to this thing. I couldn't really get out of it since I haven't spent any time with them."

Oh. *Oh.*

"And they can't really see you with me and my family, or else they'll be wondering why you suddenly have a girl-friend," I finish.

He nods. "And your family can't see me with them and not you."

"Shit," I mutter.

Suddenly, I feel bad. I've been monopolizing his time for this lie. I didn't even consider that he came to hang out with his friends.

My shoulders fall, and I drop my gaze to our boots. "I'm sorry, Rhys. This is all my fault."

"Hey." He gives me a little shake. "None of that."

His finger lands on my chin, and he tips my head back. I stare into his eyes and instantly feel calmer.

"Playing the role of your boyfriend has made this trip interesting." His grin is infectious. "Plus, I got to finger you on the slopes. No regrets there. Now, we just need to keep up appearances for your family while avoiding my friends, and I need to slip away to show my face with them. It's doable. Like juggling. Or lying to your family about being able to snowboard."

I huff with annoyance, but it's fake. I don't know how he does it, but I lose my bad mood in his presence.

"Oh shit." Rhys grabs my hand.

Suddenly, we're running.

Me and running on the slippery snow?

Is he out of his mind?

"Rhys!" I squeal. "I'm going to fall!"

"Not on my watch." He jerks to a stop and bends down in front of me. "Climb on, baby. We gotta take cover."

"What?" I peer over my shoulder, and my gaze lands on a group of people our age. "Are those your friends?"

"Yes! Now get on my back."

I climb on quickly, and his arms wrap around my calves. I squeeze tight, enveloping him with my arms. My face is buried in the crook of his neck, and the dirtiest thought slips in. *What would he do if I started to kiss him there?*

I lose track of where his hurried pace takes us. Through a

throng of people, back inside the lodge, we're immediately enveloped in warmth…then darkness.

Rhys shuts a door and moves us away from the windows.

"Where the fuck are we?" he mutters, still holding on to my legs.

I peek around, and although there aren't any lights, I know exactly where we are.

"Santa's workshop." I laugh quietly. "It's a cute little cottage that the resort has set up during the day for kids to walk through."

"Explains why my head is almost touching the ceiling," he mumbles.

I bury my face into his neck again, trying to conceal my laughter.

"Oh, you think this is funny?" he asks, amused.

A breathy laugh leaves my mouth, landing right over the spot on his neck that was tempting me no more than a few seconds ago.

"I can make it even funnier," I tease.

Before I give him a chance to question me, I press my mouth beneath his jaw and kiss him. His pulse quickly picks up speed and pounds against my lips.

"Mira, Mira, Mira." Rhys tsks his tongue while moving his head to the side to give me better access. "Are you trying to get me all hot and bothered in Santa's workshop?"

"Who, *me*?" I pepper his neck with light kisses until I get to the stubble on his sharp jaw. He turns slightly, our mouths a breath away.

"You're going to end up on the naughty list if you keep that up." His voice is strained.

And I can't help but love the sound.

I smile shyly. "Good."

CHAPTER 13
RHYS

I DROP her legs and relish the feel of her body sliding down mine. Once she has her footing, I spin to face her. I step forward, and she goes back. Her eyes sparkle, a mirth that's been missing lighting up her expression.

Fuck, she's pretty. The attraction buzzing is insane, an electrical storm crackling between us. She unzips her jacket and lets it fall to the floor.

I mirror her movements, prowling forward.

Those blue eyes of hers widen when she bumps into Santa's workshop. Without warning, I grasp her hips and lift her onto it. Part of me wants to go caveman on her, to rip her pants off and thrust into her until we're both gasping for air. I want to feel her climax around me, her breathy moans in my ear while her nails rake down my back.

The other, saner, part of my brain recognizes that we're still very much in public. Daring escape from my friends and her family aside, anyone could walk in and ruin the moment.

So…we better make use of the time we have.

Mira removes her shirt and chucks it at my face.

I barely manage to catch it, lowering the fabric to stare at her.

"We're in public."

She hooks her fingers through my belt loops and yanks me closer.

My dick leaps to attention.

"Kiss me." She tips her head back, her heavy-lidded gaze locked on my lips. "Right now."

Fuck.

I can't resist that siren call. I step even closer and lean down, cupping her jaw with my palm. Her breath exhales in a whoosh, and then my lips are on hers. I want time to examine her tits, to peel her bra off and fasten my mouth on her nipple. I want to be skin to skin, but we'll have to settle for this.

"Not enough," she whispers against my lips.

My dick is at attention, straining my zipper. I'm going to have imprints for days at this rate, since I seem to be constantly hard around her. How does she *do* that?

She seems to be done waiting for me. With strength that catches me off guard, she grips my hips and turns us so it's *me* leaning on the workshop bench.

And then she's on her knees.

"Holy bells," I whisper.

She shakes her head. "Now's not the time for puns."

With ease, she pops the button of my jeans and tugs the fabric down. My boxers go with them, and the sweet relief of my cock finally out in the open is *almost* enough to make me groan.

But I am nothing if not restrained, so I stay silent. I soak in the image of her in the shadows, the press of her fingertips into my thighs.

Her tongue flicks out, licking her lower lip.

Then, she descends.

I make a noise. I can't help it. One of her hands comes up, under my shirt, and her fucking claw-nails dig into my abdomen.

A warning to be quiet, perhaps?

I get it, I get it. But Mira takes more of me in her mouth, her tongue swirling, and then she *sucks*. Her cheeks hollow, and I see freaking stars. Way too soon—*damn it, my reputation is going down the drain with this girl*—my balls tighten, and I can't stop myself. I tangle my fingers in her hair, taking control of her motions.

My hips move, and she hums. Or moans. Either way, the vibrations travel down my shaft, through my balls, and zip up my spine.

"I'm gonna come," I warn. I force my hand away from the back of her head.

I expect her to withdraw, but she just doubles down. Her palm cups my balls.

Shit.

"Really gonna—"

She flicks her tongue, and I lose it. I hunch forward, groaning as I come in her mouth.

This will take the edge off, at least.

When she withdraws, I cup her elbows and help her back to her feet. She wipes her mouth and offers me a smile.

It's the smile of a temptress.

A *seductress*.

"Now I *really* don't give a shit that we're in public." I lean down and drag her closer.

I cover her mouth with my lips. When she parts hers, I taste myself mixed with her saliva. A strange combination, but one I'm not against.

I pop the button on her jeans and slide my hand down. Under her panties, into her hot arousal. She lets out a breath and shifts. She widens her stance, and I push a finger inside her. Her muscles grip my digit, but I withdraw and retreat to her clit.

A cheer goes up from outside, startling us both. I glance over my shoulder at the window, but it's still dark.

"Focus," she grits out.

"Yes, ma'am," I whisper.

I kiss her cheek then drag my lips down to her jaw, to her soft neck. My body hums when I make contact with her throat, kissing and licking and sucking.

Let her try to hide this evidence of us, huh?

Her hips rock, guiding me subtly in the right direction. She's just about there when, suddenly, it's like the whole room has illuminated.

Instinctively, I drag my hand away and pull her down. We both duck, frozen, until it dawns on me that the lights *in* the room didn't just come on…

It's the tree lighting.

The tree that's directly outside one of the windows.

Which means the crowd, now very visible out the other one, can most likely see straight in here.

"Shit," Mira hisses. "My shirt—"

"I got it." I reach back and snag it then help her into it. I shove my dick back in my pants and button up while she does the same.

We're still crouched in the shadows, but I wouldn't be surprised if, at *any* minute, someone opened the door and started up the workshop for the kids. Or adults. Santa doesn't discriminate.

When I look from the door back to Mira, she's staring at the tree with a sad expression.

"What is it?"

She exhales. "We missed it."

I shake my head slowly. "Nah, Frostbite. I think we got the best seat in the house."

Her expression flickers, and her gaze comes back to me.

"Come on." I hold out my hand. "Let's make a run for it so we can finally finish what we started."

CHAPTER 14
MIRA

THE DOOR SHUTS BEHIND RHYS, and silence fills the cabin. My skin is still warm from his touch, my lips swollen from kissing. There's an ache between my legs, and there's only one way that'll go away.

"What are you thinking?" Rhys stands against the locked door with a spark in his eyes that makes me feel nothing less than desirable.

This is starting to feel real.

He takes a step forward, and my inner thoughts filled with a warning fade.

Real or fake, I want this.

I repeat his question. "What are *you* thinking?"

A sexy smirk takes over his face. "I'm thinking that all I want for Christmas is you."

"So, you want to unwrap me?" I tease.

I take a step backward.

Rhys hitches an eyebrow as he watches me move out of his reach. "I want to *unravel* you, Mira."

I gulp. The mirth that is usually present in Rhys's gaze is gone. Nine times out of ten, there's a hint of humor lingering in his tone, but that's gone, too.

Rhys looks ready to devour me, and suddenly, I have second thoughts.

Is this a good idea?

He's my fake boyfriend. I all but forced him into a sham of a relationship, and now I'm excited about his fleeting touches, wishing they'd linger a little longer.

Hell, I even had the thought to force us into another outing with my family just so I can play make-believe again. That's how I know I have it bad. Wanting to be around my family just so I can be around him? *Insane.*

Rhys hums, pulling my attention back to him. "Where's my naughty little Mira hiding?" He erases some of the space I've put between us. "You seem bashful all of a sudden."

I fidget and avert my gaze. "I'm not being bashful."

When I glance back to him, he squints. His head tilts to the side. He takes another step closer and my stomach flips.

It was all fun and games earlier, but now my head is starting to catch on to what's happening between us.

As I'm bouncing back and forth with thoughts, Rhys somehow ends up right in front of me. His scent engulfs my senses, dizzying me. My breath hitches when his finger gracefully touches my chin, lifting my face to peer at him.

"I can't decide what version of you I like best," he whispers.

I swallow. "What do you mean?"

A chill races down my arms with the brushing of his thumb against my swollen bottom lip.

"The fun, flirty version of you when you're teasing me…" Rhys's hooded eyes move back and forth between mine. "Or this version… the one where your cheeks turn a bright pink when I look at your lips, because you know I want them on mine. Or how you keep nervously looking away because you realize you're starting to like the way I stare at you from across the room."

I open my mouth to deny his claims, but as soon as I try, he cuts me off with a deep, moan-eliciting kiss.

Shit.

Rhys's tongue moves over mine with purpose. He grips me beneath my butt and hauls me into his arms. We kiss until he lays me back on the bed. A shaky breath climbs from my lungs with him towering over me.

"Mmm." He shakes his head. "I know what version I like best."

My jeans begin to slip down my legs with his gentle pulls.

"What version?" I ask quietly, my voice raspy.

Rhys's fingers slowly creep up my thighs, and I tingle everywhere. The moment he hooks his thumbs under my panties and steals them, I'm practically panting.

"The one where you beg."

An argument is on the end of my lips, but it disappears altogether when his tongue swipes against my pussy.

"Oh my God." My head tips backward from the blissful amount of pleasure coursing through my body.

I was so worked up earlier, before we were interrupted, that I'm already seconds from an orgasm. I spread my legs wider to give him easier access.

"More," I moan.

I tremble when he starts to use his fingers *and* mouth. He leans back for a second, and I pout. "Let me hear you beg, Mira."

Never.

His head disappears between my legs again, and he places soft kisses to my inner thigh. My eyes clench shut when he pushes his finger into me—slow, tiny thrusts that do nothing but make me embarrassingly needy. I'm in a frenzy. I grip the sheets. Arch my back.

Oh, to hell with it.

I break.

"Please, Rhys," I whine. "I need…"

He nips my pussy with his teeth, and I lose my train of thought.

I feel his lips curl into a smile on my leg.

"What do you need, baby?"

Without hesitation, I answer, "You. I need *you*."

I quickly sit up and grip his shirt. Our eyes catch for a second before he's shedding his clothes. I do the same with my shirt and bra, tossing them both to the floor.

I sigh with relief when he centers himself between my legs.

Heat covers me from head to toe when he pushes inside. *God, yes.*

My hair fans all around me when I fall gracefully back to the bed. Rhys kisses me deeply, his tongue languid over mine with hot strokes while he tilts his hips. I shake in his grip, quiet moans and whimpers filling our quiet cabin.

"God, you feel amazing," he groans.

Moving my neck to the side, Rhys places his mouth there and sucks on the delicate skin. My insides coil with desire, my toes tingling with pleasure.

"Fuck," An orgasm rips through me out of nowhere.

Rhys pulls back and stares down at me, his thrusts growing stronger and faster.

"Tell me you're on birth control, Mira." His voice is strained and beyond hot.

Through the ride of my orgasm, I manage a nod.

"Thank fuck," he says.

Rhys pushes into me even deeper, and I watch in awe when his head tips backward from pleasure. His jaw slacks, and his muscles tighten. One more thrust and he freezes with his dick so far in me I feel him *everywhere*.

Holy shit.

Our breathing is labored, and there's a glistening sheen on both of our bodies.

As soon as Rhys comes back down to earth, he glances at

his cock still buried between my legs. He flicks his gaze to mine, and my heart comes to a stop. A smirk curves onto his flushed face.

"I'm fucking you in the hot tub next," he says.

I don't even have it in me to argue, because *yes, please.*

CHAPTER 15
RHYS

SPOILER ALERT: we do it in the hot tub.

We do it in the shower, rinsing off hot tub water.

We finish our fucking escapade on the floor because Mira won't let me fuck her on the bed when her hair is wet, which, now that we're snuggled up together under the covers, I totally get. A soaked pillow would *suck*.

"Tomorrow is Christmas Eve," Mira mumbles.

I stare at the ceiling. "Yeah."

"Is it weird not being with your family?"

I haven't really been thinking about my family. Between Mira and *her* family, and our ruse, I've been busy. Too busy. But now that I do, a hollowness fills my chest.

"Yeah," I manage through a lump in my throat.

God, what a baby I am. First Christmas away from my parents…this should be *fine*, and yet, I'm overcome with this stupid melancholy.

"Do you have traditions?"

I pull her tighter into my side. She comes willingly, inching her knee up until her leg is across my thighs. Her arm across my stomach. It's secure. *She's* secure.

"We'd always do stockings on Christmas Eve," I say. "At

midnight or however close my parents could get us to it. When we were younger, I think they lied about the time. I was probably in bed by eight o'clock so they could put out the presents from Santa and prepare for an early wake-up."

I chuckle, but it fades fast.

"Everybody contributed to the stockings. Little gag gifts, you know. Or things they had been asking for but it wasn't really a *present*. Like, one year, Mom kept complaining about losing her reading glasses. So, I got her a pack of six, and Dad got her those cords that let you hang the glasses around your neck."

'That sounds nice."

"Yeah. Then, obviously, Christmas is the presents, and all the extended family would come over since our house was the best. And my parents are excellent cooks. We'd do more presents, an early dinner…"

"You sound sad."

I clear my throat. "Well, maybe sad-*ish* over missing it."

"And you're here instead of there because…?"

The guilt hits me next. "Thorne is going to the draft, and this was our last hurrah as a friend group."

Mira sits up suddenly. Her hair swings in her face, and it's automatic to reach up and tuck it behind her ear. All it does is reveal her horrified expression, though.

"Rhys," she whispers. "I've been keeping you from your friends this whole time—"

"It's okay." I tuck her hair again and keep my palm cupped to her cheek. "We have a whole second semester together before we go our separate ways…"

"That's not the same as spending quality time—"

"They're all coupled up," I interrupt. "Thorne and his girl-friend, Briar, have probably been fucking like rabbits in their cabin and only surfacing for food and a run or two on the slopes. Same with Aaron and Willow, and the rest of them."

I don't mention the standing dinner reservations for our

group that I've been excusing myself from every night. It's a miracle my friends like to eat late, and Mira's family tends to prefer the early bird special.

"Let's talk about *your* family."

Mira groans and flops onto her back. "Let's not."

"You remind me of the forgotten kid from *Home Alone*."

She jabs a finger at the ceiling. "That's exactly who I am! Thank you for validating my feelings about that."

I grin. "Anytime, babe."

"But… it does suck. Just know that you participating in this scheme with me is making things, like, seventy percent better."

I roll on top of her. My dick has officially woken back up, and she spreads those pretty legs for me easily, making room for my body. When she feels my hardness between her legs, she loops her arms around my neck. Her knees come up, and I push inside her with little resistance. She's still slick from her previous orgasms and perhaps renewed arousal.

Talking about the woes of family and holidays can really turn a girl on, apparently.

"Seventy percent better," I murmur against her lips. "Missed opportunity for a sixty-nine reference."

She huffs.

"Let's see if this"—I pull out then thrust back in, watching how her eyelashes flutter—"can raise the bar."

———

I leave Mira asleep and head out to meet my friends. I got a rather sternly worded text from Aaron that basically said: show up or Thorne is gonna beat my door down.

Can't have *that*.

So, here I am. Exhausted and happy. Satiated. And trudging across the freshly fallen snow to join my friends for an early breakfast.

They must be fucking during the day and actually sleeping at night to get out of bed so early. *Heathens*. This is vacation!

"Merry Christmas Eve, Rhys!" Willow, Aaron's girlfriend, calls when she spots me.

She's wearing a dark-green...I guess you could call it an ugly sweater. It looks like it could fit her huge boyfriend better than her, swamping her frame. There's a reindeer on it with a red pom-pom nose.

Glitter pom-pom.

I had a run-in with glitter once. A poor prank by a girl I was dating—or, uh...fucking. Who can tell the difference these days? She put glitter in my shampoo, and it took *ages* for it to all come out.

Did I also generally use my shampoo as bodywash? Yes.

I've since learned... one, don't fuck psychos, and two, use bodywash for the body and shampoo for the hair. I've also learned that anyone who has any glitter is in the psycho category.

She comes closer, and I twitch.

"He's got a phobia," Thorne calls.

Willow pauses and turns back toward him, her brows furrowing. "What?"

He gestures vaguely at her. "Reindeer. Terrifying creatures."

I snort.

Willow faces me again, covering the face of the reindeer. "Oh my God, Rhys, I'm so sorry. What an awful time of the year for you!"

"I—" I shake my head and nod at the same time, ending up moving my head in a circle. "Thanks."

"Come on." Thorne tilts his head. "We've already got a table."

I follow him back, weaving through the tables, until we get to a giant C-shaped booth. I take the lone chair facing my pack of coupled-up friends. Thorne and Briar are closest to me, Aaron on my other side. Some of the other names and faces I should know, but they're not *my* friends.

My chest tightens.

Why the hell do I wish my fake girlfriend was with me right now?

Probably because it's not really fake anymore, asshole.

"So, who's got you cooped up in your cabin?" Briar asks.

I jerk. "Huh?"

She smirks. "We've hardly seen you, so…"

"I've been around." My tone comes off defensive.

"In between doing the horizontal tango with some girl?" Her eyebrows go up. "Or maybe *girls*?"

My face flushes. "No. I mean, yeah. No. I don't know. I've been hanging out. It's you guys who are all…"

Guilt flashes across Thorne's expression, but he doesn't say anything. Not since there are so fucking many of us. Eight plus me. Jack and Aaron are on the football team. Marley and Lydia are Briar's friends. The only person I'm unfamiliar with is Marley's boyfriend. I probably *would* know him better if I showed up to more shit, but…

"It's Christmas Eve," Lydia says suddenly. "We're spending it together as a group, right? There's some choir tonight, I think they're doing a singalong sort of thing. That'll be fun."

I swallow. "Yeah."

And yet… how the fuck am I going to get out of doing shit with Mira's family?

The waitress comes by and takes our orders, and the topic shifts from me to an incident Lydia and Jack saw on the mountain. It isn't until I tune back in that I realize they saw *us*. Mira and me.

"He had her on his back, snowboarding down the mountain. I don't know if she was injured or what, but it was cute as fuck." Lydia nudges Jack. "Would you carry me down the mountain if I sprained something?"

"Of course, baby." Jack leans down and kisses her.

Ugh. "We should've made a no-PDA rule," I say under my breath.

Thorne grimaces.

Although, it's kind of nice to know that my actions were observed and deemed *cute as fuck*. I'll have to tell Mira that.

"You gonna come up the mountain with us?" Aaron asks me.

Jack and Lydia are still kissing.

I point to them. "If those two quit it, then yes."

Marley nudges her friend, and the two separate. Lydia's face is red, and Jack seems smug. I shake my head, trying not to smile.

Ah, to be young and in love. Can't relate.

Something twinges inside me—the instinct that what I just said was very much a lie.

Oh, no.

I can't relate to that, can I?

I'm not in love with a *fake* freaking girlfriend.

And yet...

CHAPTER 16
MIRA

"SO... WHERE'S YOUR *BOYFRIEND*?" Cammie smiles deceitfully as she twirls her champagne flute. The cranberries and rosemary sway around the glass, taunting me.

I already downed my Christmas mimosa—the featured drink for brunch at the resort. I wish I had twelve more to get through the rest of the day.

"Why'd you say it like that?" I ask. "As if you don't know his name."

Cammie raises an eyebrow and shrugs.

Does she know?

My reality slips. If she knows, then that means my fake relationship with Rhys is over.

Why does that make my heart twinge?

"Yeah, where is Rhys?" Marcus asks, glancing up from his phone for the first time during this lunch.

Rhys is spending time with his friends, like he should've been doing all along.

There's a part of me that's hurt he's not here, like he chose his friends over me, but that's the most ridiculous thought I've had this entire trip, aside from the whole fake-dating scheme I came up with. If anything, I should feel guilty for keeping him from them, and I do.

I'm jealous, too.

I would rather be with Rhys right now, and not just because I'm stuck shielding myself from my family's condescending remarks in between every other bite of food.

"He's video-chatting with his parents," I finally say.

I shoot my sister a glare, fully fed up with her jabs. I don't know if it's because I've finally had enough, or if it's because it's partly her fault that I'm in this situation to begin with.

My heart is becoming invested, and it's going to end up broken.

That's her fault, too.

"Oh, really?" Eliza smiles at me from beside my dad. "Is he close with his family?"

My stepmom actually seems interested, giving me her full attention.

At least I've fooled one person at this table that Rhys and I are in a fully committed relationship.

A smile touches my lips. "Yeah, he is."

I go on and on about his family dynamic and some of the traditions that Rhys has with his family. The more I talk about him, the bigger my smile gets.

By the time I'm done, the entire table is quiet.

All eyes are on me.

Or past me?

"What? Is Santa Claus behind me or something?" I half-laugh.

Liam perks up with a crayon held tightly between his chubby fingers.

I spin in my chair, and that's when I hear my sister laugh from her seat.

Shit.

The blood drains from my face.

Rhys stands with his snowboard in his hand, face red from the cool wintery wind of the slopes. He's in the middle of his large group of friends, laughing at something one of the girls said.

"I knew it!" Cammie shouts. "You two aren't even dating… are you?"

"What? Mira wouldn't lie about something like that," my dad argues.

I turn around briefly. All eyes are on me.

Marcus clicks his phone off. "I've gotta give this my full attention."

A wave of nausea hits me. I try to come up with an excuse or cover my tracks in some way, but all I can think is, *it's over.*

I peek over my shoulder again, and as if he can feel me, Rhys looks over.

At first, his brown eyes light up with excitement. His cheek rises with a crescent smile, but then, his gaze shifts to the rest of the table, and his expression falls.

"I've gotta record this." Cammie snickers at my back.

My eyes water, and I don't even know why.

Rhys and I are at an impasse. Our stares are locked on one another from across the resort restaurant, and I wish he could read my mind.

One of his friends nudges him with his elbow, and when Rhys doesn't budge, he follows his line of sight. Suddenly, his whole posse is staring at us.

"Is that who you've been fucking?" one of them asks. His voice carries across the room. "No wonder you haven't been hanging out with us the entire trip."

My stepmom gasps.

I clench my eyes together tightly.

Could this get any worse?

"Jack!" a girl exclaims. "She's with her whole family. *Shut up.*"

"I'm confused," my brother says. "Aren't you two dating? Why don't they know—"

"Dating?" someone interjects.

"Shut *up*, Thorne," Rhys stresses.

Oh God. They moved closer.

I finally open my eyes, and Rhys is no more than a few feet from me. His lips are tugged into a frown, and I can tell he wants to help in some way, but he doesn't know how.

I shake my head and look away.

When I turn to face my family, they're clearly waiting for an explanation.

"No," I admit. "We're not dating. In fact, I hadn't seen him in years until we ended up in the same cabin by accident."

Cammie snorts while Rachel tries to hide a laugh.

"So you lied?" My mom's shocked expression clearly displays her disapproval.

Cammie makes a noise of satisfaction. "Of course she lied. I knew there was no way he was dating her."

Ouch.

I don't even have it in me to stick up for myself.

It's already embarrassing enough that this is happening in front of random strangers, but for Rhys and his friends to be standing behind me while I'm made out as the black sheep of the family is the cherry on top.

Instead of bickering with my sister, I scoot my chair from the table and stand abruptly.

My napkin, that my mother forced me to put on my lap, falls to the floor.

I attempt to flee, but stop at the last second when Rhys wraps his hand around my arm.

"Mira…" His tone is soft, like he only says my name for me to hear.

I shake my head and manage a tiny smile. "Thanks for making part of my trip bearable."

I jerk my arm out of his grasp, and he lets me go willingly. I walk out the door with my arms crossed over my chest, as if they'll be able to catch my bleeding heart as it falls right out of my chest and onto the snowy ground below.

CHAPTER 17
RHYS

FUCK.

I stare at Mira's entire family, their expressions ranging from horrified to *smug*. Snide bitches. I feel my friends at my back, but they're secondary to the judgment permeating the air. My gaze ticks from face to face, finally landing on Cammie—the meanest of Mira's siblings and, arguably, the leader of the pack.

"You're right," I tell her. "There's no way Mira and I would date."

She sneers.

I hold up my hand. "But not because I'm better than her. It's because she's the kindest, warmest person I've ever met. She cares so fucking deeply. She's a good person. She's *smart*. And for some reason, you hold those traits against her."

The table's silence only deepens.

I shake my head, my disgust unable to be hidden any longer. "I've watched you all degrade her with flippant comments all week. Why? She's your sister. You're supposed to love her, not tear her down."

Thorne's hand lands on my shoulder. He's not telling me

to back down. It's a silent show of support. Same as on the field. He's an anchor.

"This holiday trip has been nothing but a farce, but not ours—*yours*. Cammie doesn't hide her loathing, but not a single one of you sticks up for Mira." I inhale and square my shoulders. "You should all be fucking ashamed of yourselves."

Her dad's mouth opens and closes.

Her mom seems on the verge of tears.

Good.

Another part of me wants to push on the bruise harder, but… it's not worth it.

Mira is, though. She's worth chasing and pursuing and fighting for, and that's exactly what I'm going to do.

I turn away from them and shove through my friend group. They part for me, but Jack doesn't move fast enough. I catch his shoulder with mine. He stumbles, but he doesn't say anything.

He's an asshole for his comment.

Thorne follows me out of the lodge and down toward our cabin. Halfway there, he calls for me to stop.

I jerk around and hold my hands up in surrender. "I'm sorry, man. I'm sorry I lied—"

"I don't even understand what the fuck just happened," Thorne grumbles. "Want to give me the CliffsNotes version?"

"Sure." I run my hand down my face and wipe away my smile. "Mira and I were double-booked in the same cabin. She walked in on me shortly after we arrived, and we tried to fix it, but the resort was sold out.

"And of course, there's the little fact that I know her and her family. We used to be neighbors. So when her sisters walked in, shit-talking Mira without realizing she was there, it just kind of happened that Mira went and introduced me as her boyfriend."

I wince. "*Fake* boyfriend. We hashed out the details later, but… I was willing to help her out."

Thorne laughs. "Jesus, man."

"You should've heard what they were saying."

"If it's anything like the preview we got in the lodge, I understand." He steps closer. "You didn't have to hide it from me, you know."

"Yeah. I was just"—I lift my shoulder—"trying to respect her wish to keep it under wraps, even though that normally doesn't apply to you."

My best friend sighs. "This trip's dynamics are kind of fucked up with you being the only solo one, huh?"

"Oh, you noticed that?"

"I'm sorry. The couple-y ness of it got out of hand, but we weren't going to leave you out because you didn't have a girl."

I glance over my shoulder, toward my cabin. The door is shut, but I imagine Mira is in there, waiting or stewing…

"Well, maybe you have a girl now," Thorne says quietly.

"What?"

Thorne slaps my arm. "Go get the girl, asshole."

I smile. Because you know what? *Hell yeah.*

I leave him standing there and jog the rest of the way. My boots make for clunky movement, but I bound up the porch and shove the door open.

She's packing.

"You're leaving?" I blurt out.

Mira looks up. Her eyes are red, tears still on her cheeks. She sniffles and wipes absently at her cheeks, nodding slowly. "No point in staying. My family will mock me for years to come for this shit. I'll have a better Christmas at home."

"No."

She takes a breath. "No?"

"No." I go to her and take her hands, helping her rise.

"No, you're not going. No, you're not going to spend Christmas alone. *No*, your family will not mock you about this for years to come. Just… *no*."

I take over wiping the tears from her cheeks and under her eyes. I tuck her blonde hair behind her ears, hating that she's been suffering—even if it was just for a moment. A heartbeat of suffering is too much for my girl.

That's right, I said it.

"This isn't fake," I declare.

Mira scoffs. "It's been fake—"

"We've lived under the pretense of it being fake to hide from the sexual tension," I interrupt. "But we got *that* under control yesterday, which means all that's left is the relationship stuff."

"The relationship stuff," Mira repeats. "No, Rhys, I think you knocked your head on the trail or something. There's no relationship, remember? We just jumped into bed together—"

"Mira Winters." I cup her cheek. "Respectfully, babe, shut up. I'm trying to tell you that the fake shit no longer applies to us. It was quick and unexpected, but I find myself head over heels for you. I'm pretty sure I'm falling in love with you —if you'll have me."

Her mouth opens and closes. Her eyes are even more blue with the sheen of tears, which is ridiculous, but there it is.

Butterflies flutter in my chest. Damn, *butterflies*? I just admitted to love, and she's crying again. I can't quite tell if they're good or bad tears. More spill down her cheeks, and I wipe them away. She's not telling me to get lost, at any rate. That's got to be a good sign.

The longer she remains quiet, though, the more nervous I feel.

"I've never felt like this about someone before," I whisper. "Please say something."

Her hand comes up and covers mine. "Yes. Yes, I feel it,

too. You and me. The… the realness of it. I'm falling in love with you, too."

"Thank God."

Then, I do what I did from the beginning. I lean down and kiss her.

CHAPTER 18
MIRA

HIS MOUTH SOOTHES each of my wounds. I left him standing there in the resort restaurant with the shocked expressions on my family's faces and immediately had the notion to get the hell out of dodge.

Only, Rhys came to my rescue *again*.

He pulls away long enough to push my shirt up and over my head before gripping my face and kissing me. I place my hands on his shoulders and jump up, knowing he'll catch me. I wrap my legs around his waist and he backs me up to the bed. He lays me on my back and tugs my pants off quickly, like he can't touch me fast enough.

"Rhys." I sit up on my forearms and watch him tug his own shirt off. "You're not just saying all this because you feel sorry for me, right?"

Shock crosses his face. His hands freeze over the button of his pants. "You think I'd do that?"

I glance away. "Well, no… but—"

His pants hit the floor, and next thing I know, he's climbing over top of me. "You're so used to people tearing you down that of course you'd think that…" A line appears between his eyebrows. "Don't worry, Mira. As your boyfriend, it's my duty to make you see your own worth."

Butterflies fill my stomach. "Boyfriend," I repeat.

Not my fake boyfriend. My actual boyfriend.

He shrugs sheepishly. "Well, yeah. Unless you want to get hitched and really blow everyone's minds."

I quietly laugh with a roll of my eyes.

"Mmm, do that again." Rhys nips my lip with his teeth. "I love it when you roll your eyes at me."

He moves closer to me, and a wistful sigh escapes. His tongue sweeps inside my mouth with a hot kiss, but he backs away at the last second. "I already told your family off. It'd be fun to put a ring on your finger and really make them hate me."

I freeze. "You told them off?"

He chuckles, pressing his hips forward. "Hell yeah, I did. No one treats my girl like that and gets away with it."

I grow warm, not only because I feel his hard length between my legs but because I'm beyond flattered that he stuck up for me.

"Thank you," I whisper, gazing up into his eyes.

He grins. "You're welcome."

I gasp when he pushes into me. My eyes flutter, and my body buzzes. I expose my neck, tilting my head to the side, and he takes the bait by running his nose along my jaw. When his hot breath hits my ear, goosebumps rush to my skin.

"Now, let me fuck you so good you forget all about them, yeah?"

A whimper leaves me as he slams into me harder. "Mm-hmm," I moan.

"That's my girl."

A knock sounds on our cabin door, and we still.

My eyes grow wide.

"Who is it?" Rhys shouts, the veins in his neck straining while he holds himself above me.

"It's Rachel." There's a quick pause. "And Cammie."

"Go away!" I shout.

Rhys starts to move above me, clearly on the same page as I'm on.

"We want to…" Cammie's voice trails.

"Apologize," Rachel finishes for her.

Rhys scoffs. Our eyes clash, and when I grin, he mimics it.

"Sorry," he says toward the door. "We're busy."

I don't hide my moans. I spread my legs wider and arch my back. *God, it feels good.*

Everything is heightened. My skin is itching for his touch everywhere.

"I want you to moan extra loud," he whispers in my ear. "So they get the point."

"Mira," Cammie says my name again.

She *clearly* isn't getting the point.

"You're going to have to wait—" Rhys's voice strains, his angle deeper.

I moan loudly but not because he told me to. It just feels *that* good.

"Are you two fucking?" Rachel's tone is more of a shriek. "Oh my God!"

"Good work, baby." Rhys winks at me and snakes his hand between my legs. His thumb presses against my clit. "Now it's time for the grand finale."

By the time it's all said and done, I think the entire resort heard me.

CHAPTER 19
RHYS

WE SPEND Christmas with my friends. I don't want Mira to waste another second on her idiotic, hateful family. I don't want her to spend her *holiday* feeling any sort of judgment.

My friends? My family? They don't judge. Okay, maybe Jack. But he has a bruise on his jaw—courtesy of Thorne—to dissuade him from any more comments.

We're all packed into a corner of the second floor of the lodge. We can see the top of the lit tree out the huge windows, and there's a fire crackling. There are a few other groups up here, but Aaron and Willow came up early to snag the best seats.

I relax into the cushion, my arm around Mira. She's talking to Briar, seated next to us, and every once in a while, I pinch my leg just to make sure I'm not dreaming. After a whirlwind yesterday of yelling at Mira's family, making her scream my name over and over in our cabin, and sneaking out to the lodge for a late-night bite to eat by ourselves… it's Christmas.

And I got the girl.

Best. Christmas. Ever.

Last night, huddled under the blankets, we discussed the

future. We spoke in hushed tones, like it was some fragile thing to protect. *Our* future.

We could do long distance for this last semester then get a place together.

Yes, that's fast. But… I mean, when you know, you know. Right?

Part of me doesn't even want to wait that long, but there's some tiny piece, deep in my chest, that's terrified of rushing this and ruining everything. I've never felt this way about someone—and so fast. Mira is like some damn Christmas miracle.

"Time for presents!"

Mira stiffens. I meet her wide-eyed gaze, confused about her sudden anxiety.

"What is it?" I whisper.

"I didn't get you anything," she replies under her breath.

I try—and fail—to withhold my laugh. I kiss her temple. "Obviously, babe. Neither of us could've predicted this. Would it make you feel better if I said I didn't get you anything?"

She nods and presses her lips together.

We watch Thorne gift Briar some pretty earrings, and Willow give Aaron a new tie and socks—which is how you know they've been together the longest, in my opinion.

"The second you start giving me socks is when I know we're out of the honeymoon period," I say in Mira's ear.

She giggles.

"Not that I'm complaining about that," I add.

"I've seen your vacation socks." She pokes my thigh. "You could use some new ones."

"Gee, thanks."

"I'm just saying, if that's what you picked to bring on *vacation*…"

"Yeah, yeah. I've been a little busy." I roll my eyes.

"Wow." Thorne's awed voice interrupts our conversation.

He pulls out a hand-painted canvas of him and Briar, his lips parted in shock. "This— Briar—"

"Merry Christmas, Cassius." Her voice comes out low and raspy.

"God, that's a sex voice if I've ever heard one," I say.

Thorne ducks down and catches Briar's lips. I should look away, and yet I find myself staring as the kiss deepens. I catch a hint of tongue—

"Get a room!" I shout. I lean forward and cover Jack's eyes. "There are kids watching."

Mira elbows me.

Jack shoves my arm away.

Thorne flips me off, but at least they stop kissing.

I sit back and grin. All in a day's work.

Finally, it seems like things have come to a close. The chatter turns to the upcoming semester, the games left on our schedule, and…

Gosh, am I really going to be saying goodbye to Mira in just a few days?

"Come with me," I blurt out.

She stares at me in shock.

"I mean, you know, we can find you something to do in Shadow Valley, right? It just seems silly to waste time…" My mouth dries. "Unless you want to stay where you are. That's fine. I didn't mean to assume that you should drop your life for, um… for that. For me. Not that you would be—"

"Rhys," Briar interrupts. "Jesus, shut up and let the girl answer you."

All eyes are on us, and I swallow. This was the wrong place to ask her this. It was very impulsive, too.

"Talk me through this," she says slowly.

"You pack up and move in with me. We can find you a job, or maybe you take a class if you want, or…" I'm fucking sweating. "I don't know. I just know I'd rather figure it out with you than not say anything and constantly wish you were with me."

Mira's expression is *stoic*. Like, she's giving me absolutely nothing.

Then, miraculously, a smile creeps across her face.

"Okay," she agrees.

"Okay," I repeat. "Yeah. We're doing this."

She holds out her hand, and I take it. Instead of shaking it, like she expects, I bring it up to my mouth and kiss her knuckles.

She laughs. "Merry Christmas to us, huh, babe?"

Best Christmas ever.

Epilogue: Mira

One year later

Christmas in Shadow Valley is nothing like back home. Not only am I welcomed with open arms by Rhys's parents, but their house is calm and cozy. The scent of pine fills the air as Rhys's mom pulls me into a warm embrace. His dad shuts the door behind us and pats Rhys on the back, which quickly turns into a hug.

It's been a while since we've seen them.

Rhys is smack-dab in the middle of football season, which means there isn't a lot of time for leisure travel. We're lucky that we're even able to spend Christmas with them. We flew in this morning, and we fly out this evening. The quick trip is worth it, though. The smile on Rhys's face is genuine, and with his mother doting over us, we may never leave.

I follow after her and answer all her questions about the online classes I've been taking while Rhys and his dad discuss the rest of his season.

"Where are you two going after this?" his mom asks.

I tune everything out as soon as I step into the living room. Rhys surely answers her question, but I don't hear a thing.

"Wow," I whisper.

Rhys wasn't kidding when he said that Christmas with his parents was the best thing ever.

I half expect Santa Claus to come down the chimney at any given second.

Rhys's arms come around me and I fall back onto his chest.

"I told you. Pretty cool, huh?" he says.

I scan the garland on top of the mantel with a ridiculous number of ceramic Santa Claus figures lined up perfectly. I smile at the thought of the Christmas gift that we'd purchased in the airport for his mom.

Nothing like last minute.

Rhys said she'd love to have a Santa who was dressed as a pilot, and I argued.

But now that I'm standing here, staring at her collectables, I take it back.

A warm fire crackles in the fireplace, coating my cheeks. I move closer to the Christmas tree. I softly run my fingers over the cute years-old handmade ornaments from the guy at my side.

"Oh my gosh," I giggle. "Please tell me this is you."

Rhys's cheeks turn pink, and he pinches the bridge of his nose. "Come on, Mom. Really?"

"Don't be embarrassed," she says. "It's cute."

"It's not cute," he grumbles.

I smack his hand when he reaches for the rabies-looking hand-drawn reindeer with a picture of him as a child for the face. It's hilarious. And okay, fine. It's cute.

He was a cute kid.

I hope our kids end up being as cute as him.

Butterflies fill me at the thought. I want to do the same

thing Rhys's mom did. I want our tree to be filled with their cute Christmas ornaments from over the years.

I'm not pregnant. We haven't even talked about something like that. If I wasn't on birth control, I probably would be, considering Rhys can't keep his hands off me.

Would it be a bad thing?

Kids. With him. Christmas morning with rosy-cheeked kids tearing into gifts.

"Why are your cheeks red?" Rhys furrows his brow.

"Huh?" I roll my lips. "Oh, I don't know. The fire is… warm."

I've been with Rhys long enough now to know that he doesn't believe me.

His mouth hovers beside my ear, his voice low and raspy. "Were you having a dirty thought, Frostbite?"

I snort. "From looking at your creepy reindeer? No."

"Then why are you acting jittery?" His nose grazes the side of my jaw.

I quickly glance at his parents, but his dad is organizing the gifts under the tree, putting them in piles for Rhys and me, while his mom scurries off to the kitchen.

"Wait." Rhys leans back slightly. "Are you feeling uncomfortable because you've never had a Christmas like this?"

A laugh bubbles up out of my throat. "You mean, am I feeling uncomfortable because Christmas with your family is more like stepping into a Hallmark movie versus Christmas with mine where it puts *Home Alone* to shame?" I shake my head. "Not at all. This is perfect."

"Then what is it?"

I scan the room again, the soft glow of the tree lights warming me from the inside out. Presents are piled high, and mistletoe hangs above the archway leading into the kitchen.

"Babe?" he sighs. "We should've flown to see your family last night, huh? Christmas Eve at your parents'—"

I quickly interrupt him. "That's not it."

I glance to see his dad helping his mom with the coffees she's grabbed for us. They stop under the milestone and kiss. I turn back to Rhys, his warm brown eyes searching mine. "I want this one day," I admit.

"Want what? Christmas at my parents'? We will spend every Christmas here if that's what you want."

I smile. He's always so willing to do anything to make me happy.

"No." I shake my head. "I mean, yes. But I'm talking about this…" I nod to his parents, to him, and then to the living room. "I want kids and a warm, inviting home. I want Christmas morning to be as magical as it feels right now with little spitting images of us, opening presents, feeling loved and cared for."

Rhys freezes with his hands intertwined in mine.

I search his face, afraid I said too much, but then that amused grin slides onto his face, and I breathe again.

"Spitting images of us?" he muses. "Like, you want me to give you a baby?"

My lips twitch with a smile. I shrug and act cool. "Two."

His eyebrows shoot up, a flirty glint twinkling within his eyes. "Two babies?"

"Babies?"

Rhys keeps a hold of my hands but snaps his attention to his parents. His mom's eyes are wide with shock.

"No!" I shout. "I'm not pregnant!"

Before he even opens his mouth, I know exactly what Rhys is going to say.

"Not yet," he wiggles his eyebrows and moves us under the archway.

I tilt my chin and see the mistletoe above our heads before looking back at him. His parents are chatting excitedly in the background, but my gaze never wavers.

"You've gotta marry me first," I tease.

Rhys bends low, his lips grazing mine. "Good thing I already have a ring."

"A ring—"

Before I can question him any further, Rhys kisses me deeply, both of us uncaring that his parents are feet away, discussing what they want to be called when they become grandparents.

In the *very* near future…

The End

Check out the rest of the Shadow Valley U universe here!

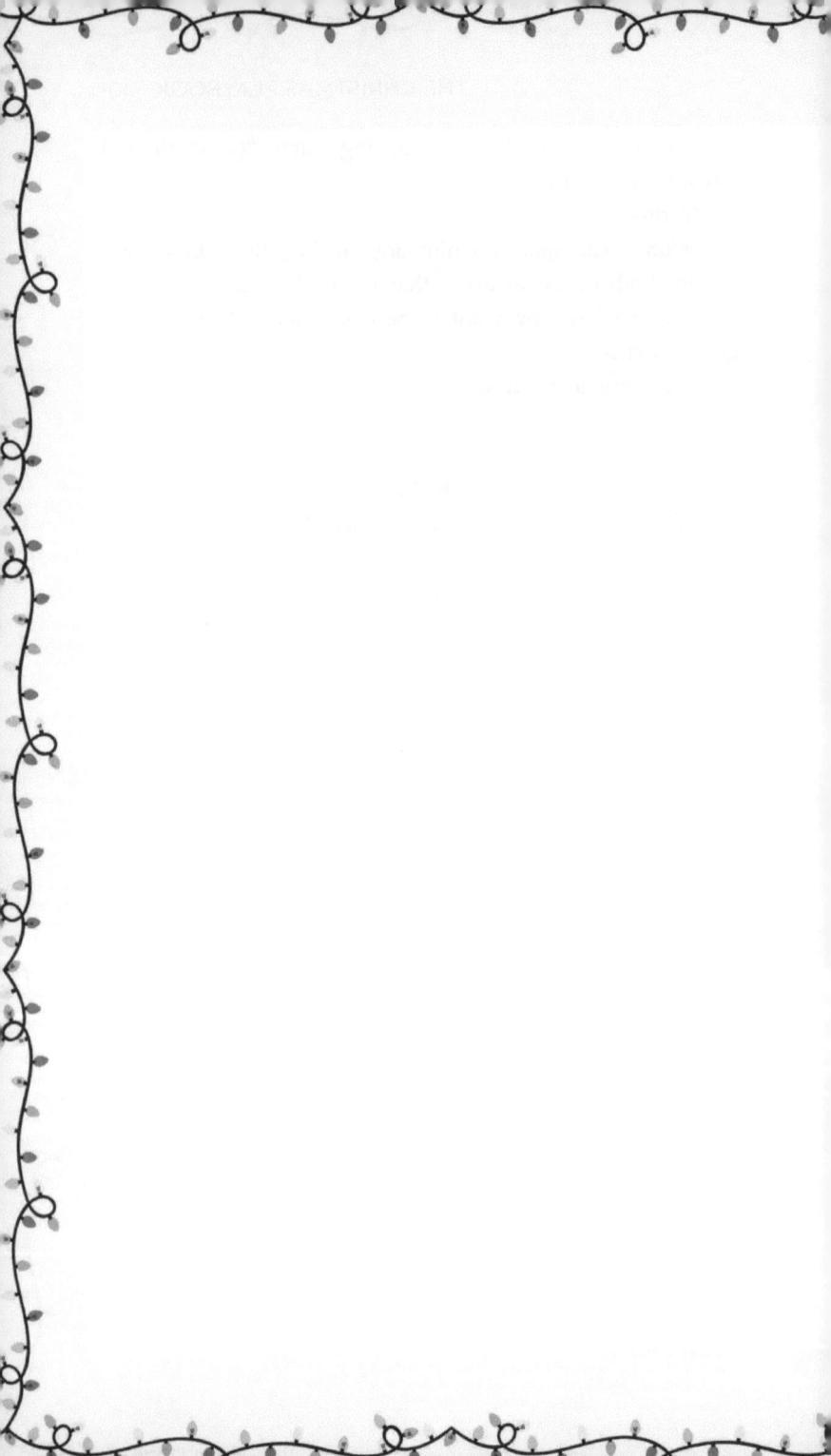

ABOUT THE AUTHORS

S. Massery is a dark romance author who loves injecting a good dose of suspense into her stories. She lives in Western Massachusetts with her dog, Alice.

Before adventuring into the world of writing, she went to college in Boston and held a wide variety of jobs—including working on a dude ranch in Wyoming (a personal highlight). She has a love affair with coffee and chocolate. When S. Massery isn't writing, she can be found devouring books, playing outside with her dog, or trying to make people smile.

Join her newsletter to stay up to date on new releases: http://smassery.com/newsletter

S.J. Sylvis is an Amazon top 50 and USA Today bestselling author who is best known for her angsty new adult romances. She currently resides in Arizona with her husband, two small kiddos, dog, and cat. She is obsessed with coffee, becomes easily attached to fictional characters, and spends most of her evenings buried in a book!

Join her newsletter to stay up to date on new releases: https://www.sjsylvis.com/newsletter-signup

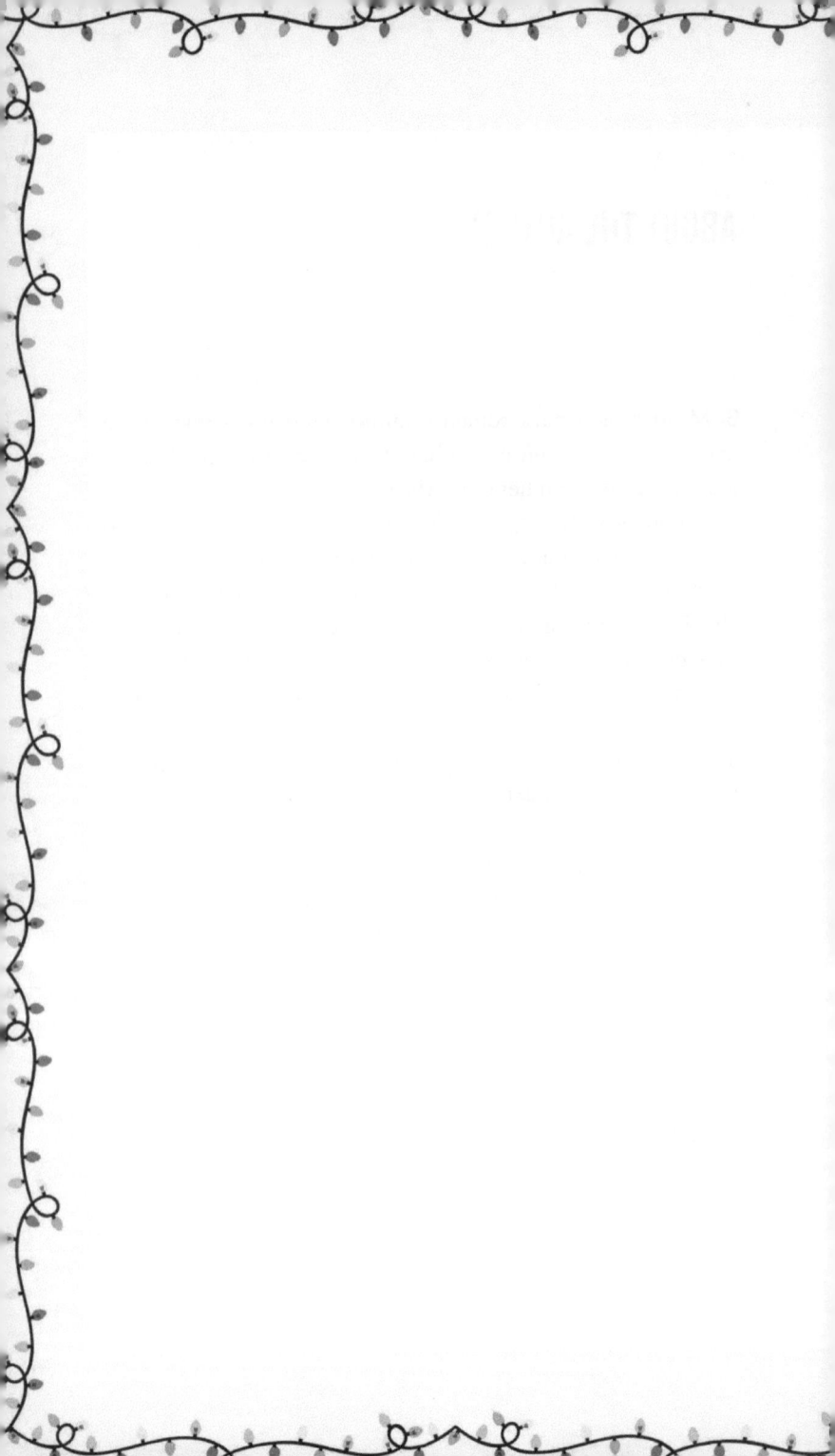

ALSO BY S. MASSERY

Sterling Falls

#0 Thrill

#1 Thief

#2 Fighter

#3 Rebel

#4 Queen

Sterling Falls Rogues

#0 Terror

#1 Nemesis

#2 Warrior

#3 Martyr

DeSantis Mafia

#1 Ruthless Saint

#2 Savage Prince

#3 Stolen Crown

Broken Mercenaries

#1 Blood Sky

#2 Angel of Death

#3 Morning Star

More at http://smassery.com

ALSO BY S.J. SYLVIS

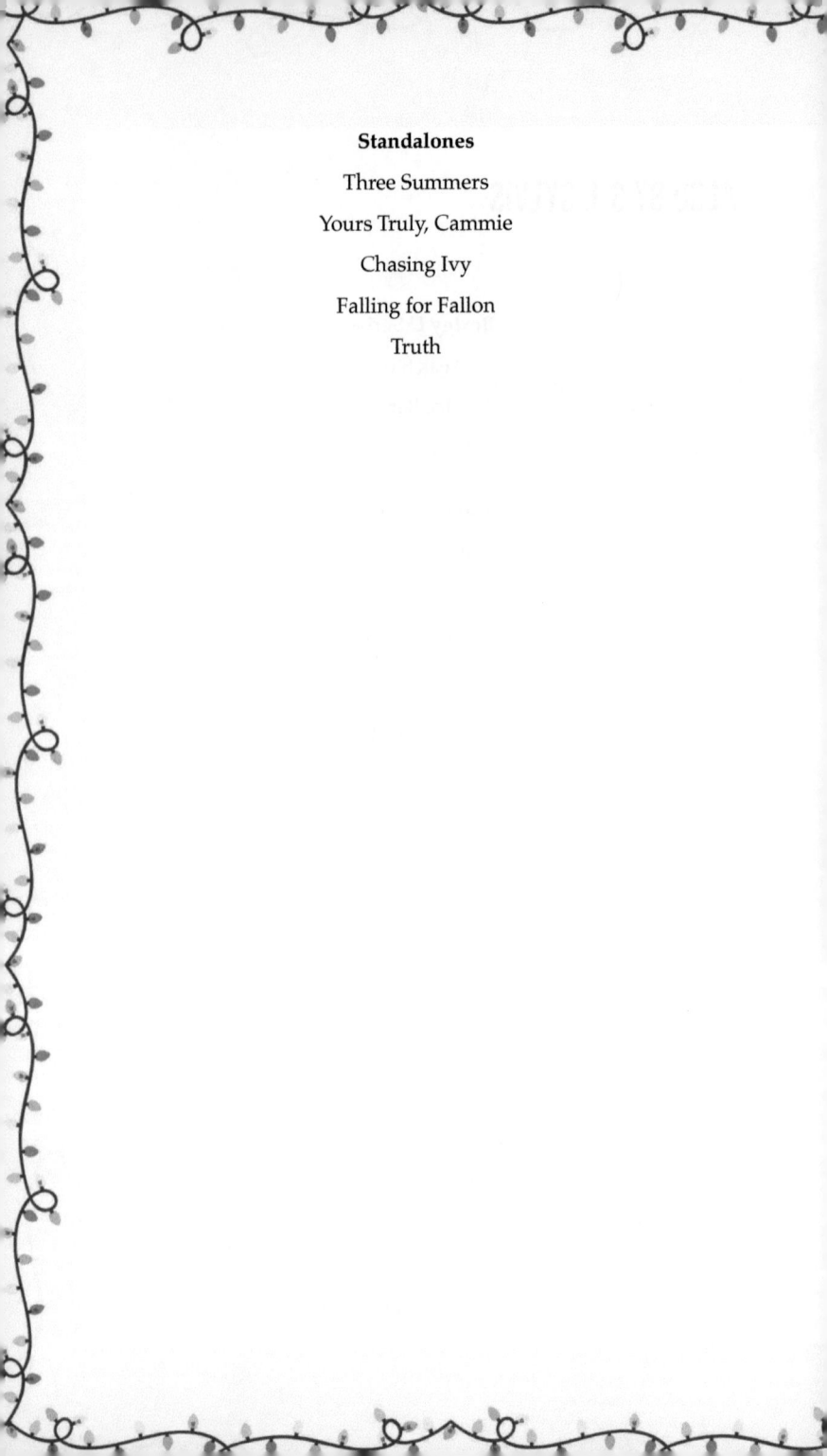

Printed by Libri Plureos GmbH in Hamburg, Germany